ELJI AND THE
GALRASS

THE ESSENCE SAGAS BOOK ONE

COLIN SINCLAIR

World Castle Publishing, LLC
Pensacola, Florida
Copyright © Colin Sinclair 2018
Hardback ISBN: 9781629899381
Paperback ISBN: 9781629899398
eBook ISBN: 9781629899404
First Edition World Castle Publishing, LLC, June 25, 2018
http://www.worldcastlepublishing.com
Licensing Notes
Cover: Karen Fuller
Editor: Maxine Bringenberg

Table of Contents

PROLOGUE

They rose, the dark, the keen, and the bright. Each to offer words of comfort and solace to hearts that would embrace their message, as they had done each day from the beginning of time. Only now, in amongst the tumult, a different voice could be heard, a voice intermingled with the others, a voice giving a message of inclusion and agreement. It was not possible to see from where the voice came. It had no color, no light, no dark, and no form. It had not grown from, nor was it interested in politics, in gender, in race. Once it was a single voice among many. A choice given, a chance to embrace something new, yet as old as the universe itself. It didn't offer power, or riches, or status. Yet it held a tone all of its own, a promise of equality, fairness, and truth—a vision of eternal peace, harmony, and rest. When heard, its resonance was that of the human soul, and for each new soul that heard the voice its message became clearer. On that morning, and on every morning thereafter, as it had from the very beginning of time, it spoke. At this time, for human kind it had become a choice, gaining in volume and intensity.

It was humanity's hope, as it had always been, as it was the hope of all creation.

He watched, shifted by a phase in time from the world of humanity, as he had watched for millennia the conflict that this race seemed to thrive on. At times he had been tested to the limits of his ability to not interfere in the lives of humans, the race he had helped to create. He had been sure, on no less than a dozen occasions so far, that they would obliterate themselves. But at each stage, the soul's message that he had buried deep within the subconscious of all humanity had managed to avert complete disaster.

He had wept to see his creation turn from the truth, and he had wept to see them show the spark of understanding that had made all the other life forms in the universe coalesce into a society of caregivers and shepherds of all living things. There was still time and there was still hope, and at this juncture it did seem to him that the balance was turning toward understanding.

He had never before witnessed a race that had such a fierce independence of soul that could harbor such love and kindness, and yet could accomplish such atrocities. Never before in all his limitless life span had he seen such passion and lust for doing evil in the name of good. He reflected on the times he had spent amongst this race as one of them, and how this had felt....

CHAPTER 1
ELGRED AND CHARINA

The morning was bright, hot, and a slight breeze eased through the room. He turned over and slid himself from the bed, conscious that he didn't disturb her as he got up. He walked over to the shutters that opened straight onto the winding streets and opened them. The noise of the day was just beginning to increase in intensity. He could hear the hawkers moving around, pulling their carts and setting up stalls for the day's trade.

He stared at the cobbled streets, and as he did they came alive as the breeze caused the sand to eddy amongst the stones and cracks. Mesmerized by the twisting dance of the sand, he watched, seeing in it the complexity and beauty of life itself. It always astounded and amazed him, the simple way nature took hold and forged its own direction.

He waved his hand and removed the invisible barrier that he erected every night so as to stop anyone from entering the house. It also had the added benefit of stopping the sand, but allowing in the breeze to keep the internal space cool. He stood and breathed in the air, tasting the promised heat of the day mingled with the aromatic spices that filled the narrow streets with their subtle yet alluring aromas.

He knew she was behind him even before she slid her arm up under his and onto his chest from behind. As she pulled herself in, he felt her soft form touch his skin and marveled at the feel of it. She rested her head on his back and pulled in even closer; he never tired of that feeling. In fact, they had both been amazed at the unexpected joy that just touching each other in this human form brought to them. It was an unexpected benefit, indeed, of being in a solid state of reality. He sighed and turned his head to gaze at her. Leaning back and to the side, his lips met hers and they kissed, the soft soulful kiss of two beings that understood each other, inside and out.

She disentangled herself from him and walked across the room, turning back with a smile that made his soul leap. She moved through the curtained doorway at the end of the room, and he turned to stare out of the large windows. His eyes scanned the scene in front of him, and his mind turned back to the situation they were in. They had created this situation to try and get the message to begin to take hold even further, knowing that what they did now would have a massive impact on humanity in the future.

They had come close to what was considered direct intervention, which was frowned upon by the few of them that had responsibility for life in the universe. Still, he felt the gamble was worth the risk, and doubted his motives would be questioned. After all, this world and this life form were his creations, and he had nurtured them so far, well within the bounds of allowable intervention. They showed the most promise of all life they had created…perhaps as time progressed they could even find one that would become part of them, a being that these humans called "gods," those with the power to create and destroy all known things. It was his true hope.

He turned and followed her through the curtained door and headed for the streets of Mehem.

When they had come back to this time they had found a thriving civilization, but fractured by the greed and wealth that power could bring. Those that could had risen to subjugate others and enslave them to do their bidding. It had taken him and Charina a few decades to start to make them see the benefit of a society led by respect and sharing, but they had made progress, all be it slowly.

To begin with, on an almost daily basis they had provided what might be considered small miracles to move things in the right direction. Simple things at first, like the ability to build shelter that stood the test of time. Teaching people how to construct and use the natural resources. How to divert water to areas that now fed hundreds, and how to grow sustainable food that was plentiful for all.

Their hardest task so far had been to get these people to understand the benefit of working together in numbers. To do this they had had to give them something to believe in. This was the glue that forged alliances between people, and which gave them the desire and direction to collaborate toward the greater good.

That something was, for all intent and purposes, a "God," a benefactor, but one of the people. They had given him the title of "Bremen," and had ensured by the proliferation of stories and writings that he was known and well regarded for his benevolence and love of his people. He ruled over the city that they were now in. They had revealed themselves to his father many decades ago, and it was him that helped them begin to share the message. Bremen himself was young, bright, and loved by his people.

CHAPTER 2
FRAMIN

Framin lifted his hands from the strands that connected him to the world. He had spent the dark hours on this world following the vibrations and viewing his work across the globe. Each of his followers was connected to him through this web of vibrations, and he could influence them by just having a thought and transmitting it.

How easy it had been, he mused, to find people that would succumb to his will. He had only to show them the pleasures that could be achieved by connecting with him and the powers they gained from those connections, and they were willing to accept his control.

Oh, how simple these people were, so driven by the gain of worldly goods. He was so pleased that they did not have the concept that all the things he provided them with were just a tiny speck of the real benefits they could achieve by embracing the powers wielded by Charina and her cohort Elgred. Elgred's power dwarfed the things that Framin could do. Framin's one advantage was that he did not care about the constraints within

11

which Elgred worked. He cared not who he upset or what rules he broke. He had already been cast out, and his only concern was that his activity did not allow them to find him before his plans had a chance to work.

His one burning desire was to control all that they created, to turn them to his will, to gain the power back that had been stripped from him. He intended to do this by utilizing the collective strength of the human race, and to harness all of their greed and hatred to elevate him back to true power.

He leaned back in his throne, a thing of opulence and beauty, designed to awe all those that saw him. Fashioned with power from the majestic grehonaught, a being of power, wrath, cruelty, and greed, but able to induce exquisite pleasure at need, it presented itself to those that saw it in the shape of the thing they most desired but feared, each seeing something different yet magnificent. The rest of the room was adorned with gold and encrusted in fine jewels fashioned into artefacts that took the breath away. Framin had endowed much of these decorative pieces with energy from the universe, which meant their appeal was more than their outward appearance. The walls themselves he had fashioned so that they also appealed at a basic level, and they changed appearance and color depending on who was looking at them. In essence he had created the whole room to be the best possible room any person could imagine.

He himself stood as tall as any man, well over 6 feet 5 inches, with shoulders and arms that looked powerful enough to crush bone and rock. His skin presented itself in a burnished bronze color that almost glistened. His face, high browed and lean, was breathtaking in its beauty, and was adorned with eyes that were the color of the clearest sea, shifting between the purest green to the deepest blue. His body rippled with muscles that exuded strength, coursing as he moved in a constant flow that mesmerized the eye.

He sighed, a satisfied smile spreading across his face. "Viyana" he called, his voice emanating as if in song, irresistible and alluring. "Viyana, bring food, bring drink."

He was hungry and thirsty; it was one of the drawbacks of being human, he could not sustain himself on the energy that the universe provided—it just wasn't sufficient—and he needed to consume actual food for sustenance. He found he had a liking for some of it. One of his favorites was the local ale. It was earthy and rough and robust, and it sated his thirst whilst leaving him wanting more, a most pleasurable taste indeed.

Viyana appeared from behind the throne, a line of servants following carrying steaming salvers of fried meats and hot vegetables, sending out smells that pulled him into the present and into the time. The servants placed the salvers on the central table and disappeared, not wishing to be there too long. They knew better than to be there for what happened next.

Framin walked toward the table and began to produce beautiful yet haunting singing, discordant tonal notes, and as he did, around the table other beings started to coalesce, wisps at first but hardening as he continued to "sing." By the time he had made it to the table they were all in attendance....his twelve Gouarong, humans made strong and given powers from him due to their devout belief in his vision of the future of human kind. Twelve beings determined to bend all of humanity to subjugation and rule as servants of "the one."

CHAPTER 3
ELJI

The day was bright, the tall grass moving like waves on the ocean, yet softer and more gentle, calming in its very nature. From his position on his back, Elji could see the clear blue sky through the tall grass. His walk from the home he shared with his mother and brothers had been, as usual, uneventful, and had taken him no longer than half an hour. He knew that he had time to spend looking to the sky and envisioning great beasts in the small clouds that floated by — beasts of great power and strength. He couldn't stay there long though; he had to collect the mushrooms from the edge of the wood and return home in time for his mother to have them in the stew she was preparing, so that when his brothers returned there would be food for them to eat.

He was the youngest of his family — a slight boy, though he contained a wiry strength. His jet-black hair was shot through with streaks of silver and sat wild on top of his head. No one knew where the silver had come from, and it was of great interest to those in his village because of its unusual nature.

Some in the village said that it was a result of the death of his father when he was born; others said it was because he had been touched by the gods, and yet others still said it was an omen of dark powers. In any case he didn't care—he was not concerned with such things. A boy of sixteen summers had other things on his mind, and all of them were about the creation of great deeds and strange beasts. He was indeed a daydreamer, and was told so on nearly a daily basis.

He closed his eyes and drank in the warm sunshine, listening to the grass rustle as he drifted into his world of beasts and heroes. Something cold and wet on his face brought him back out of his reverie, and he opened his eyes to look up at a hairy face and long tongue just above his nose.

"Aker," he squealed. "What are you doing here?"

The dog barked and jumped back, and then went for his face again.

"Stop it! Leave me alone, you great beast." He laughed and got up to his feet. Aker was excited, jumping up and down at him as if to say, "I found you, where have you been, where have you been?"

Elji was sure he had left the dog tied up outside the house, but then this dog was able to extract himself from anything and find Elji. It wasn't that much of a surprise, and in any case he was always happy to see him.

"Come on then, let's go collect these mushrooms." He set off at a loping canter towards the edge of the field, the dog nipping around his ankles, to where the trees lay and where he was sure to find the mushrooms in the dappled shade at the edge.

He didn't like the forest much—it had a foreboding presence that hung around it—but he was happy to skirt the edges and collect what he could. There were many stories amongst the villagers of people going into the forest never to be seen again, but his mother had told him they were just tales told by the elders to stop children from going in and getting lost on its many winding paths. Still, he didn't like the feel of the place, so there was no danger of him venturing in. He didn't need the tales to stop him from doing that.

He slowed as they neared the edge and stretched down his hand to stroke the dog. Feeling for his belt, he undid the small sack he carried with him and pulled it open, ready to put his day's findings in.

There was a small bridge he had to use to cross the stream that ran around the edge of the field before the wood, and when he stepped on it, it creaked and strained at even his insubstantial weight. He wondered at its construction, as it seemed to just hang over the water and not be anchored anywhere, but it had been like that as long as he could remember, so he wasn't worried about it.

He turned to look at his dog, who on every previous visit had refused to cross the bridge, and was surprised to see him coming across with him. "You OK boy?" he asked, and Aker turned his head sideways and looked at him as if to say, "Why you asking me that?" Elji chortled. "OK, if you're sure." Then the dog was off, darting into the woods as if he had been spooked from behind.

Elji stopped, puzzled. His dog had never done that before, not in all the years they had been coming here. He had never shown any interest at all in going into the woods — in fact, quite the opposite. He looked up and was about to shout the dog's name when he saw a faint glow from a little way into the woods, pulsating and coming from one place. It would brighten and then dim, and as he watched from the edge he noticed that it was increasing in intensity. He could hear Aker barking. Again unusual! His dog could not be described as a barker.

He glanced back and up at the sky, and could see that the sun was beginning to lower itself; he must have rested longer than he thought. With a sense somewhere between unease and excitement, he decided to go in after his dog and see for himself what the light was. He still had time.

The woods were darker than he thought they would be, but not dark enough to cause any real concern that he might stumble. He pushed on, following the sound of Aker's bark and glimpsing the light between the boles of the trees. In front of him was a clearing, and there, somewhere near the center of a circular opening, he saw Aker looking at the ground and digging with his front paws, moving around and digging again, dirt flying up in all directions.

"What is it boy?" he asked. "What have you found?"

He walked towards him, and as he did the light disappeared…no more pulsating. Strange, he thought as he reached his dog. He looked down to see where he had been digging, but couldn't see anything other than dirt and leaves. He bent down on one knee and reached out his hand to brush away all the dirt and leaves thrown up by his dog. Nothing—very strange. Where had the light come from?

Aker had his head tilted to one side again, and was letting out a quiet sort of whine, almost like a cry.

Elji felt foolish. "OK," he said, "come on then, let's go. There is nothing here, and I don't want to be here when it gets dark. Come on, Aker."

He turned away, and just as he did he glimpsed something right at the edge of where the dog had been digging. Dropping to his knee, he reached for what he had seen.

A stone — black, as deep as night and smooth and round, and warm to the touch. He had never seen anything like this before around where he lived. It was as smooth as glass, and fit in the palm of his hand as if it were made for him. He turned it around in his hands, moving it about, and as he did he found himself being drawn into it. But it was just a stone — a different, unusual one, but just a stone.

He was about to throw it away and dismiss the whole episode, but he just couldn't take his eyes off it. Something made him place it in the sack he used for carrying the mushrooms.

"Let's go," he said again. "We need to get back."

All of a sudden he and Aker were standing just outside his village, his sack full of mushrooms, and the sun had risen a little in the sky again, as if he had misjudged it when he was near the forest. He looked down at Aker, and the dog looked back as if to say "Don't ask me."

He reached into his sack and rummaged around to get the stone. Pulling it out, he looked at it again. He began to shake. Something, he thought; it must have something to do with the stone. Confused, disorientated, he heard his mum's voice.

"Elji," she was calling. "Elji!"

"Here, Mum." he called back, and pushed the stone deep into his pocket and started to walk towards the house. He would look at it later.

He walked through the village and down the path leading to the door of the small wooden house where they all lived. Despite the fact that it was almost the smallest house in the village and needed some work, it was still his home and he loved the walk to the door, through the vegetable patch where his mum grew most of the food they needed. He could hear the chickens and pigs and the goats out back as they rummaged around in the small field they rented from the innkeeper for their livestock. Well, by rented, he meant his mother paid the innkeeper with fresh meat, vegetables, milk, and eggs that she got from the livestock they owned.

His mum, Abriana, was a strong woman, with jet black hair, a small frame, and a face that was earthy yet held its own beauty. Abriana could be a difficult woman at times. Their circumstances had dictated it — she'd had to bring up Elji and his three brothers all on her own since their dad's death. She was entitled to be hard — it had been a hard life — but at the same time she always had time for them all, and could be soft and compassionate at need Mainly though, she brokered no nonsense, expected them all to do what she bid them to, and expected them all to contribute to the upkeep of the family.

His brothers were triplets, all born within an hour of each other, and were five years older than him. It had taken his mother five years, she always said, to recover from the birth of the triplets.

They were already in, all sitting around in one of the three rooms they lived in, the room that passed as the kitchen and their main living room. His brothers were big, round shouldered, and long legged. Their faces, though, were always smiling, and they were kind and generous of heart, always teasing him; at the same time, he was sure they loved him. It was a fine family to be part of; it was a happy house.

Every day his brothers walked the two miles to the edge of the village to be taken by cart to the limestone hill, where they worked digging and cutting stone. The stones they hewed from the rock were massive, and each one was taken away, they were told, to provide for the building of monuments for the gods.

19

Most of the villagers worked in the quarry in some capacity. Each night as they finished they would leave the stone, and by the time they returned in the morning the stones were gone. In their place was a stack of gold coins, spices that they needed, and food that they couldn't grow themselves. The foreman and owner of the quarry would share out the payment, keeping a little more for himself as the owner, but ensuring that everyone got their fair share. It was a strange kind of happening, but it had now been going on as long as most could remember, and the village had become used to it as part of life in general.

Every now and then someone would try to stay through the night to see what happened to the stone, but on the times they tried no stone was taken and no payment was received. So after dark the quarry was not to be visited by anyone, and was considered out of bounds.

"Have you brought the mushrooms for me?" his mother asked.

"Yes," he answered, and was about to tell her what had happened when something hit the back of his head and fell to the floor. His brothers erupted in laughter and he looked down. A small apple rolled away from him, and his hand shot to his head. "Hey!" he shouted, startled by the sharp pain, and he rubbed the back of his head with his hand. He turned and could see his brothers laughing and smiling at him.

"You should have been back ages ago. Daydreaming again, were you?" asked Gwilliar.

"No, not daydreaming. Something happened — something strange."

His brothers laughed, looking at each other and shaking their heads.

"Yeah, we know. You were slaying one of your mythical

creatures, no doubt!"

"No! Really, something happened."

"Enough," came the sharp tone from his mother. "Now, Elji, just give me the mushrooms, and you three leave him alone."

Elji passed the bag to his mother and moved off still rubbing his head, feeling sorry for himself.

"Go and feed the animals, Elji, while I finish dinner. Come straight back and get washed up. And you three — go and get rid of the day's dirt!"

He walked out of the house, still rubbing the back of his head, and made his way to the animals, grumbling as he went. Aker appeared at his side and walked along with him. He rounded the corner of the house, walked into the barn, and sat down on the dried mud. He was certain that the lump on his head was growing at an alarming pace, and he needed to work out a plan to repay his brothers for such a slight.

As he sat the stone in his pocket pushed into his leg. Elji stood back up and took it out of his pocket, once again turning it over in his hands and looking at it. Now that he had it somewhere he could study it carefully, he noticed that while before it had appeared to be jet black, in reality it was laced with tiny lines and sparkles that threaded their way through the stone in a lattice. It was most odd; they seemed to sparkle and flux as he looked at them. He touched where he thought one of the lines reached the surface and slid his finger along it, and with that he felt a rush.

Elji dropped the stone and looked up. He was somewhere else.

CHAPTER 4
DREGAR

The inn was the center of life in the village. Jeelan the innkeeper had inherited the inn from his father, and had embellished and grown it over the years to the point that it was known by those who travelled the route as a place to visit and receive a warm welcome, with good food and great ale. The inn itself was situated between the two big cities of Mehem and Karber, and as such was used by everyone that travelled the route between the cities. Jeelan, his wife Reeanne, and their daughter Ingria were kept busy night and day serving food, cleaning rooms, and looking after the wellbeing of the patrons.

This afternoon, though, the inn was a little more quiet than usual, and Jeelan was in a good mood. Trade had indeed been brisk in the last week or so, and his wife and daughter, he thought, could do with a break from the daily routine. He looked around the large comfortable room on the other side of the bar to see if he could see them and tell them to go have a rest, but at that moment they were nowhere to be seen. As he scanned the room he noticed one of his regular travelers at a table in the corner. He hadn't seen him come in at all, but that wasn't unusual; he often just noticed him sitting at a table. Still, it was good to see him returned. He was an odd character, he kept to himself, but he always paid in gold and always ate and drank plenty. Jeelan could remember the time his father had introduced them when he was a boy, some twenty-five years past, and Dregar looked no different today than he had that first day; he seemed to be ageless. He always travelled alone, and always carried his stick and nothing else. They had talked from time to time, but about nothing of any consequence other than just gathering news. Dregar was a traveler, and had stories from the cities and from further afield. Now that Jeelan thought about it, though, he hadn't seen him for quite some time, so perhaps a catch up was needed—just to see what he knew.

***

Dregar could see Jeelan looking at him, and he knew then that the innkeeper was coming across to see how he was and what he knew. The problem was that Dregar could feel someone close by was tugging at the universal lines, and he may need to leave at any minute. Many moons ago Elgred had asked him to keep his eye on this village. Elgred expected that a young boy he had met there would have an important role to play in the future of the world, and as such it was an important job.

Dregar knew the village in any case. As it had been his stop over point for centuries, he had seen it grow from a few sparse dwellings into a thriving village. Once he knew that Elgred wanted the boy watched, he had drawn some energies into the earth around the village, and had made sure that calm and positivity was felt by everyone that entered, ensuring, as much as he could, that nothing untoward or unexpected would happen. Just this afternoon, though, he had felt a tug, and had

23

transitioned himself here to just outside the village as soon as he could. Something had disturbed his energies, and he wasn't sure what it was so thought it best to be on hand to investigate.

Now Jeelan was coming across, and he could do without the disturbance in case he needed to leave on short notice. He rose and met him halfway from the bar, extending his hand with a gold coin.

"Good to see you, Jeelan. How long has it been now? Thanks for the ale and the food, but I must be on my way. Give my regards to the wife and that beautiful daughter of yours!" He backed away, heading for the door before Jeelan could answer.

He had just got himself outside when he was jolted by a shift in his energies surrounding the village again. This time he knew it was a rift—someone had moved to another plane. Strange, he had not felt the presence of any of his kind here, or for that matter any kind of disturbance in the essence that would indicate any interference.

He rounded a corner and settled himself down beside the green space in front of the inn, but just out of sight. Closing his eyes, he stretched his inner thoughts outwards, feeling as he went. He was drawn to the boy's house, the livestock barn to be precise, and he felt the residue of the shift. He scanned the area for the boy but could not feel any trace of him anywhere. That was very strange; where was he? He was certain he could feel his essence trail. Something had happened, something unexpected, and he needed to know what it was.

He cast his energies back along the current timeline to the barn, and discovered where the boy had been sitting in the mud. Twisting his mental capacity, he followed the essence of the boy's movements backwards through time. Each being in the universe left a trail in the energies they disturbed that lingered for some time before it was absorbed by the whole. This way he was able to follow the boy back to the woods, and the clearing where he had knelt beside the hole dug by his dog.

Dregar replayed the scene and saw the boy lift the stone, look at it, and then put it away.

How could that be? Dregar knew in an instant what the boy had found. Where had the galrass come from? Had Elgred placed it there for future need? If he had, Dregar was certain that he would have said something.

In any case he needed to talk to him about it. If he hadn't placed it there, something or someone was playing with their timeline, and disturbing a possible future outcome.

Dregar stood, twirled his stick in an intricate pattern, and was gone.

CHAPTER 5
ELJI, DREGAR, AND THE GALRASS.

Nothing…there was nothing, and the weight of the nothingness was threatening to crush him. His breath was failing, he felt like his bones were crumbling, and his brain was trying to push out through his ears and escape. He was dying, he knew it, and the weight of that knowledge threatened to crush him even more quickly. Elji took what he knew was his last breath, and as he gasped, there before him was a man. The weight had gone, and he was suspended in the nothingness. Besides the vague outline of the man he felt rather than saw in front of him, there was just a void, empty and noiseless.

"It's OK, Elji," Dregar said. "I have you, we are safe. I have created an atmosphere around us that will sustain us for as long as we need, which shouldn't be too long. Once we have worked out what has happened."

Elji was so confused—what had happened to this day? Just this morning he had been leaving to go to the wood—a normal day, something that he did as part of his normal life. Now he was with a strange man who he only felt, someone he couldn't see, and was in some place he knew not where. He had come very close to death, and now he was being told he was OK. He was not OK....

"I am not OK!" he shouted. "I AM NOT OK! What's happening? Where am I?" Tears had begun to stream down his cheeks. He began to shake uncontrollably, and on thinking about it, he was sure he had wet his pants. He was not OK — he was not OK at all. "Who are you? Where are you? Where are we?"

Dregar snapped his fingers and a glow began to appear around them, but it did not extend too far. "We have to be careful," Dregar said. "I don't want to upset the equilibrium here by bringing physical matter to the fore."

"What are you talking about? Who are you?" Elji sobbed.

***

Dregar knew he had to do something and do it now. Coming to this plane of reality when you were prepared was bad enough, but to be cast here without knowledge could be fatal. It was entirely possible that Elji would lose his mind. He made a decision, and despite the possibility of physical damage, he placed his hand on Elji's shoulder and shifted them again. This time back to the reality Elji knew, but a place well removed from the village.

The place was still very dark and again Dregar snapped his fingers, bringing light to the room they had arrived in. Elji started again and bolted upright, and as he did something fell to the floor. Dregar bent down and picked the object up.

"What is happening to me" Elji screamed. He was nearly unhinged. Dregar again put his hand on his shoulder and Elji collapsed into a heap — he had passed into an induced sleep. He would control him there from here.

At least he had managed to get the galrass from the boy, and wasn't about to let him have it back anytime soon, until he knew more about what had happened. He did know though, that he couldn't keep it from him for long, and it would only find its way back to him. If he had managed to use it at all it was his for eternity. He thought about it for a moment and wondered whether he should reach out for Elgred. No, at this point he felt like he could control what was happening. And in any case, he was certain that Elgred would have felt the changes in the essence that had been caused by the events. If he was needed Dregar was sure Elgred would already be there of his own accord.

***

Elji felt like he was floating. A soft gentle voice seemed to be calling to him, and it was soothing in its tone. He didn't seem able to feel his body at all, yet that didn't seem to bother him. OK. He was comfortable, calm—confused, yes, but something felt right deep in the core of his being.

"Elji," the voice soothed. "Elji, it's OK, you are safe—I am with you. Know that no harm can come to you here. I will explain everything to you. You and I are in a safe place. Nothing any stranger than this is going to happen now." He heard a chuckle. "I suppose in the overall scheme of things, this is about as strange as it gets." Again a chuckle. "But let me help you, let me try and tell you what is happening."

His surroundings started to coalesce, and he thought he recognized where he was. He seemed to be back in the field of grass, the low sun warming him and the familiar sound of the rustling grass bringing some normality back to his mind.

"How are you feeling now?"

Elji managed a few words. "I'm OK. I feel...how did I get

back here?"

"I just want to be sure, before I start to explain, that you are OK. I am going to be standing beside you in a moment, and I don't want it to come as too much of a shock. Are you feeling calm?"

Elji nodded, and then just beside him was the man he had seen and felt earlier—but this time the situation didn't feel quite as threatening. He looked at him and realized he had seen him before at the inn in the village, a number of times. He remembered Ingria telling him, when he had asked about the man, that he was a regular traveler to the inn, and when he was in the mood to talk he had news of happenings well beyond the two cities, and of lands and people no one in the village had ever seen or ventured to. At the time this had interested Elji, and he wondered if this man knew of or had seen any of the people and creatures he had been told about in stories. In any case, it comforted him to know that this was not a complete stranger, and that knowing seemed to calm him even more.

"OK, so where should we start? Let me first start by telling you where you are. To keep it as simple as possible, the best way to describe this is that you are asleep and you are inside your mind—a kind of dream. You seem to have stumbled across something earlier in the day that has led you to these events. Do you remember the stone? It is called a galrass."

Elji did indeed remember the stone, and without thinking he reached for his pocket, but it was no longer there.

"I have it; it fell from your pocket and I picked it up for safekeeping. I will hold on to it for now. Tell me, what do you know about where you live?"

"I live in the village of Nebaril."

"Yes, but what else do you know about where you live?"

Elji thought for a moment. "Well, the village is somewhere between the two cities, and many, many weeks' journey from the river of Arl, where there are said to be more great cities. Though no one I know has ever ventured there, and no one that has passed through the village has come from those far off lands."

"And what do you know of beyond that river? And beyond what is beyond that?"

Elji thought again. "Once we had a storyteller pass through the village from Karber to the east, and he told tales of a land inhabited by people who were fierce warriors, that worshipped a great beast called a grehonaught. He said that this place was across a vast lake, and beyond a range of mountains so tall that the tops reached into the clouds. He was laughed at by nearly everyone, but I always thought that his stories sounded real." He thought a little more. "Then other tellers would preach of men who worshipped a god, and travelled far and wide from lands unknown to spread word of his deeds and kindness. I know of Bremen and how he tells of gods beyond our understanding and reach — gods who watch and benefit us. He says they live in the stars, and that he has been put here to spread their teachings and their ways. I don't understand such things. How can anyone live in the stars?"

***

Dregar was surprised that a boy so young could have assimilated such information and remembered it. It bode well for what he was about to tell him; perhaps this task would not be as difficult as he'd first thought.

"Let me tell you this — where we are now is removed from your world in time and in distance. Though I told you that you were asleep, we are really in a different place. We can do this

30

one of two ways; we can talk and the telling of the truth will take years, though back in your village only seconds will have passed. Or I can show you how to use the galrass, and it will reveal knowledge to you as you need it during your life, and we can cover the basics now. Yes, yes, I think that is the way we will proceed.

"Here," said Dregar, and he handed the stone back to Elji. "Be careful you don't run your fingers on it, and try not to spin it around in your hand. It will make you feel like you should do this — that is in its nature — but try to resist and be patient, and listen to what I tell you. Now, I want you to stare into it, and notice that though on first glance it seems flawless and black, there are lines and specks in it all interconnected. Can you see that?"

Elji took the stone and stared into it. "Yes" he said. "I see lines, and what seem to be little specks moving down the lines and around to others. They are hardly noticeable unless you look really hard. I saw them when I picked the stone out of my pocket in the barn."

"Good, that's good," said Dregar. "Now roll the stone in your hands and look again."

Elji did as he was told. "The specks seem to be moving quicker, and they are sparkling a little."

"That's it — yes that's it. You seem to have the knack. So what do you know about the stars?"

"The stars?" asked Elji, surprised by the sudden change of direction in the discussion. "They are in the sky."

"Yes, but what do you know of them?" asked Dregar.

"I'm not sure what you mean." He thought for a bit. "I have been told many things. Some say that the stars are the souls of the dead...spirits. Some say they are the gods watching. Some

31

say they are balls of fire, massive and hot."

"Well, the last description is closer than all the others, though it's a little more complicated, as all things are. You should know that in reality, everything you see, touch, and feel, and even think, is part of everything else. So there is some truth in the stories that each star contains either a god or what you would consider as the dead...." He chuckled. "Never a simple answer — always a complication till you understand the whole."

Dregar stopped and chose his next words so as to be as clear as possible about what he was saying. "What you see in the sky as stars are made up of other suns, like the one that shines on this world, and other planets that surround those suns. There are countless numbers of these in the universe, so many that they are not known by anyone. These are collected into galaxies, and galaxies are collected into clusters. Because there are so many, it means that there is always more than one reality, and therefore more than one timeline.

"Everything we know is made of energy, and energy makes everything, even you and me. Even the stones and the rocks. Then there is time. Time is something that is made up by sentient beings who have a desire to know their lifespan — it is not a real, tangible thing, but a construct. Then there are planes of reality, like the one we are in now. A different place, but the same deconstructed from what you perceive as time.

"The galrass is all of that, which I have explained, but in the form of a stone. What you have to try and understand is that because of the size and number, all possibilities exist, and that includes 'the everything' we know duplicated in multiple places. These stones are rare, however, and controlled by very few people in the universe.

"If you utilize the stone in certain ways you can move

yourself from one place to another, and indeed from one time frame to another. What we talk of here is complicated. Under usual circumstances it is saved for scholars, and beings who have studied such for millennia. I know you can't possibly understand it all, but as an idea I hope you can understand that what you know to be real is just one version of what is possible, and all things are possible if you but know how to manipulate that which makes up everything."

Elji stared at the stone in his hand and lifted his head to look at Dregar. He had a million questions, but they seemed so hopeless when he tried to get them out. He spluttered and stopped and spluttered again.

Composing himself, he said, "So you are telling me that I live here, but I also live in the stone, and I also live in everything else? How is that possible? Is that why sometimes in my sleep I see things not of this world, but of the tales I have heard?"

***

"Well, yes and no," replied Dregar. "Your sleep allows your mind to access that which your conscious does not allow. But because you have no comprehension of what is possible, your conscious does not allow it to be anything but a dream. Without knowledge and training of the possibilities, your mind would unravel and you would return to the essence of the universe. Some humans are more adept at accessing parallel realities, and you seem to have some innate ability in this area.

"When the 'Ones' created the human race, they put pathways in place in the minds of all the living entities on this planet that could be removed slowly as the race progressed in knowledge and understanding. The hope was, and indeed is, that these barriers can be erased in some distant future to allow understanding and harmony to prevail across all life here on

33

Earth.

"We are here now at a crossroads in this timeline, and events are unfolding that will lay down a possible future. Whether that future is hope or ruin depends on the human capacity to want to access the right path. Know this, Elji — you seem to be mixed up in the unravelling of that future, and from now on your path is with me, and the others who serve alongside of me to ensure the outcome that is desired. It is a dangerous road, and you have been brought to it for a reason I do not as yet understand.

"I can tell you, though, that there is a choice. I can remove you from the path, erase the past and memories of what we have spoken of, and place you back at the moment outside the forest. You would have no knowledge of any of these happenings, and you could continue your life as before. But to me you were brought here for something greater than that, and your chance here is to be bound to the future, and do something that is so good it will fill your being with power and love beyond what you can imagine."

"Will I get to see beasts?" asked Elji. "Will I see some of the things of which I dreamt?"

"Yes, Elji," chuckled Dregar. "Yes, you will."

"Then I am with you."

The mind of the young, thought Dregar, had a way of prioritizing things that was sometimes lost on those that had been around for centuries. He smiled at the thought, and hoped he had done what Elgred would have expected him to do. He would find out soon enough. He decided that they should go to Mehem to talk with Elgred, and that they would make the journey there by traditional means, as this would give him the opportunity to teach Elji things he thought he should know.

CHAPTER 6
SALOORA

Saloora was hunkered down behind the bales of cloth, her whole body as relaxed as it could be considering the predicament she was in. She was confident that they didn't know where she was—she had run through the twisting streets very swiftly and had turned and doubled back as often as she could so as to ensure they had not been able to follow her. Still it was right to be cautious—the men following her seemed to have some kind of insight. She had only just escaped them on numerous previous occasions as they had managed to track her down well beyond what she would consider to be normal ability. She was, by any stretch of the imagination, a warrior of immense ability, who understood and was able to escape even the most capable of trackers. She had been trained well and by a very unusual source. Her mind turned inwards….

She had been born seventeen summers previous and, as was the custom in the warrior tribe she belonged to, she had been abandoned in the wild hours after her birth, left in a cave beyond the reach of all other humans to either thrive or die as the gods willed it. Less than one in a hundred survived this ordeal. For the first few days of her life she had screamed as babies do, hungry and tired and cold, but he had visited her and placed his hand on her and quietened her, staying for no more than a few minutes, but on his departure she knew what she needed. She had cried no more, and had, with the power of some basic understanding, used her mind to pull on the universal fabric and draw to her the cave lioness. From that animal she had suckled and grown, and had learned the ways to hunt and track and be as one with her surroundings. She had very quickly become accepted by the pride as a whole, bending them to her will with her understanding of the basic nature of the fabric of the universe.

Seven summers later she had left the pride and made the journey to return to her order. She had been welcomed back, and had taken her rightful place among them as a trainee warrior. Even at that early stage she knew she surpassed even the leader in her abilities and understanding. She became known as "Ahhbreshemen," voice of the god, though still she preferred her name of Saloora, a name taken from the sound of the cave lions cry in the night as they kept track of each other. It hadn't taken long till she left them again to discover her true calling, and find the one who had given her life and set her on the path that was driving her.

A noise behind her and to the right alerted her. She snapped out of her thoughts and her body tightened, coiled, ready to answer any threat. It passed; perhaps a rat or a small rodent scurrying through the bales looking for nesting material or food. She closed her eyes and extended her mind, gently probing her surroundings and stretching out down alleyways and streets. Nothing…she could not feel them nearby.

For the last week or so in this small city she had felt somehow that she was close to finding him. The sense of an impending meeting and the fact that her abilities seemed to sharpen day by day, as if they were being lent power by something else, confirmed her intuition.

She eased with cat like grace from her crouched position, her movements lithe and subtle, flowing like water over rounded stones and with a fluidity that denied human constraint. She came to rest again at the corner of a junction and hunkered back down.

It was then she felt the hand on her shoulder, and her whole mental capacity shifted. She was transported to another plane, and in an instant she knew she had found him—or rather, he had found her. Her whole being felt like it had expanded to fill the universe, and she felt in touch with every living entity.

Everything suddenly snapped back. She realized he had removed his hand, and then she looked up at him.

Elgred smiled at her, a smile so pure and wonderful it filled her whole being.

"You found me!" she said.

"Come on, follow me," he said as he walked past her. She followed without question.

She looked at him again. This man—he felt so familiar, but how could it be that she knew him after all this time? She knew who he was, she knew his purpose, and she knew it was him that had visited her when she was only a few hours old…how could that be?

"It's because I felt you," he said. "That day you were left in the cave, your soul cried out and I found you. When I touched you, I opened your mind and showed you what is possible. I knew that one day we would meet again, that you would seek me out, and that together we could begin to strengthen our cause."

"How did you—?" she asked.

"Because you are part of me and I am part of you, there is no need for us to voice our questions. We are part of The One, and as such we understand each other at a basic and fundamental level. We have no secrets. You can't hide anything from me anymore than I can hide anything from you, and that is how it should be. I imagine you will be hungry—let's find somewhere to sit and eat, and you can tell me how you came to be here. It's always much better when spoken rather than me looking into you…it seems to carry so much more color when the tale is told. Come, let's sit, eat, and talk." He seemed genuinely pleased at the opportunity, and she was indeed hungry.

He looked at her again, and she saw his eyes shift from green to blue, and saw the whole of creation seated there. She was sure—now she was sure she was safe, she had found him, and her true journey would begin.

He led her down a few twisting streets and they came to a door adorned with the image of a brass coffee jar, decorated with mother of pearl handles and jade insets so that it glistened in the early morning sunlight. Elgred pushed the door and they entered through a small, low ceilinged passageway, and exited into a bright, plant filled courtyard. The edges of the room were filled with multi colored tasseled cushions and low wooden painted tables that were dotted around. Each table had silken cloths and small brass platters filled with liquid, upon which floated either bright open flowers or small sticks and yellow powder. Under the platters were small candles that were keeping the liquid warm and causing it to emit the smell of spices and the scent of exotic blooms.

They sat at the nearest empty table and settled back. A man appeared and asked their pleasure.

"Coffee—thick, spiced, and black," Elgred said. "And could we please have some of those amazing cinnamon rolls and some cheese?"

Saloora realized she was famished. It had been days since she had eaten, and now it was an option. Her stomach started to complain to her for lack of attention.

"So tell me how you made it here. The last time I saw you, as I said, was in the cave when you were but a few days old."

Saloora took a deep breath, cast back into her mind, and began to tell her tale.

She remembered awareness coming over her and a man walking away and knew that she had to reach out with her mind and get some help. A distress call came from her mind asking for food, and that thought stayed in her mind. She heard a soft padding and felt a rough tongue rubbing across her face, and then something soft surrounded her and lifted her up, twisting her around and placing her back down. Her face then seemed to be surrounded by the same softness, and she could smell something sweet. Without having to think her mouth sought out a nipple, and she suckled and tasted the fluid. She sucked harder and kept sucking, swallowing in gulps that filled her stomach. That was the start of her association with the cave lioness that had come and saved her life.

Over the next few months her vision cleared. She got stronger and was able to move and shuffle around, her growth was prodigious, and what would normally take a human child months to accomplish she managed in days, soon learning that she could stand on her legs, and then that she could shuffle along, and then that she could walk. Very soon she was following the lioness out of the cave and into the mountainous area that surrounded it, catching mice and other rodents, biting off their heads, and devouring them in chunks. She grew stronger and quicker once this skill was achieved.

Months changed into years, she told him, and with each passing day she became more aware and was able to join the lioness on all her journeys, ranging across the mountains. Sometimes they would see others of the lioness's kind, and sometimes other creatures that predated, but always she stayed hidden from their sight. They worked together as she grew, cornering larger and larger prey until she could hunt and bring down an adult mountain goat. She had learned to communicate with growls and noises, but somehow she also had a connection with this wild beast through her mind, and they both knew what the other required.

Time continued to pass, and as each day went by she became more sentient. Soon a feeling settled in her mind, a feeling that was pulling her somewhere new, somewhere she knew her adoptive mother could not go.

"I knew at that point I had to leave and head back to find others of my kind. The only thing I knew for sure was that there were others, but I didn't know where, so I thought I might start my search back at the cave.

"Once back at the cave I followed what I thought was a path for a few days, and soon I came across a building and I hid. I spent the next few weeks living around the edge of the building. Soon I was able to see that they were clothed, and during the dark I managed to take clothing that was suitable— but I continued to watch and listen. My mind easily grasped the language that the people used, and I learned what seemed to be acceptable behavior. I practiced the sounds on my own at night away from them.

"It was as I was sitting one night practicing the words that Dregar came. I hadn't heard him, and in the next second he was just standing in front of me. Dregar took me then, and together we wandered from building, to village, to city, and back to village, and as each day passed he taught me what he knew. There is much detail to tell of how things happened and of places and people, but the tale is long and needs telling in its own time.

"As my seventh year came Dregar took me back to where he said I had first entered the world—a warrior tribe of women living near the foot of the hills of the cave. He said I should go back and learn of my tribe and how they lived.

"It was evident to me that these people, though my descendants, were primitive in their knowledge of the world and its practices, but I learned from them their use of weapons and their beliefs. It didn't take me long, and by my sixteenth year I was ready to move on again. Something was driving me on; of course, I now know that this was a calling to come and find you. I reached this city two weeks ago and sought to learn as much as I could, and in the doing I seem to have stumbled across some men who were less than pleased I had disturbed their hideout. They chased me many times when I took food or drink from them. It became a game, and that is where I was when you found me. Hiding after relinquishing them of yet more food."

She smiled and looked at him again. The coffee arrived, and along with it the cinnamon rolls. The aroma was amazing. Elgred poured the coffee, spooned some honey into the thick black liquid, and passed it to her. She sipped. Though it was hot, the taste exploded into her and filled her with what could only be described as pure pleasure. She could see that Elgred was having the same experience. He laughed inside her head. *Amazing stuff, isn't it?*

She hoped then that the rolls were going to bring the same experience, and they didn't entirely disappoint her. She thought that if she hadn't had the coffee first these would have been amazing in their own right.

They both fell silent and just enjoyed the time of eating and drinking.

"When you have finished, I have something to show you and someone I would like you to meet," Elgred said, "and I am sure he will be delighted to meet you."

They sat for a while drinking the coffee and eating. When they had finished he stood, and she followed him again out onto the street. Her life was beginning, she knew it. She could taste the promise.

CHAPTER 7
THE TELLING AND GATHERING OF THE TWELVE

Framin sat and looked round the table. What he saw was, in essence, twelve versions of himself, all of them less in stature and with less power. Though he had taught each of them how to harness power from the fabric of the universe, each had been given only a glimpse, and to each one a different use had been taught, dependent on the land and the people they belonged to.

He had been clever. These Gouarong were the same twelve he had taken to his cause hundreds of years ago, but at differing stages in time he had let them go as if in death, and had renewed them again, wiping from them the ability to harness what they had learned beyond what he had taught them.

The danger with giving beings power was that they lusted for more, and if they were clever enough they could learn themselves. The last thing he needed was to have Gouarong that had ambitions above their station—he had to be sure he had complete control over them. So far, with the exception of a few incidents of over ambition, his plan had worked well. The balance was difficult; he did need them to have a relentless urge for power and destruction, but he needed them to understand the futility of challenging him.

Each was staring at him as he took his seat, and each had the look of men of power and men used to being obeyed. He had left them alone too long, he knew it—he could see on their faces that some of them had thoughts of grabbing his position and installing themselves as the ultimate ruler. Now was the time to put a stop to that. No time like the present.

"Before we eat and before we discuss what is next to be done, I have something to show you all."

In front of each an orb appeared, and in each orb a vision of a woman and a child. To each of his Gouarong, Framin was showing them the wife and child he had ensured they all had. The women were strong and powerful looking, and each had a boy some fifteen years old at her side; strong boys, regal and proud, images of their fathers in stature and bearing. As they watched the images they could see energies emerge and surround each of the boys. The fields of energy began to contract, and each of his Gouarong could see fear on the faces of their offspring, and they could see the mothers frantically calling for their retinues. The energies continued to contract, the boys faces began to contort, and though they could hear nothing they could see the screams in their minds. The lines of the energy field shifted and began to glow and burn, continuing to contract. Each line in the field sliced through the boys like hot knives through butter. Within seconds all that was left of each boy was a charred pile of skin and bone. Mothers and their retinues stood stock still, aghast at the scene before them. The orbs snapped shut.

Framin took a moment to allow the vision to infiltrate the minds of his Gouarong. "I needed you all to understand something fundamental. Each of you is given what I CHOOSE TO GIVE; each of you has what you have by dint of my desire. That you contemplate you can take my place has caused you to kill that which is yours, yet given by me. There is no future or past where you can usurp my will. If ever you think again that you can challenge me, the same fate will befall all you have built and hold dear. I don't need you. I utilize you because it saves me energy, but I don't need you. Do I make myself clear?"

At that Framin looked around the table, staring at each and ensuring that the fight had drained from them.

A collective breath could be felt, and "Yes, lord" was voiced by each. One by one each of them stood, placed hands on their chests, and with a twist of their hands they pulled their hearts from their bodies and held them towards him—a display of utter subjugation. He held them then, letting them weaken by this deed; they couldn't keep this up for long. He waved his hand then, giving them permission to return to life.

Each sat, and though they had witnessed such a scene and had given him their allegiance, they still wore the bearing of those that would broker no interference in their plans. They were in the end ensnared by the power they had been given, and it controlled them like a drug.

"Each of you now has a task. It is time to step up the plan to totally ensnare the masses you control. You must complete the construction of the universal line portals within the allotted time I have given you. I will visit each of you in turn at that time, and your subjects must be conditioned to sacrifice themselves at the given time. Then and only then will you reach the godhood I have promised. Then and only then will you sit at my side as equals.

"The energy of misery and doubt must be released into the

world—it must breed avarice and greed and malice. It must overpower the lattice of hope and good that Elgred is creating. Once and for all we will have an end to hope, and once and for all we will live as gods, subject to only our own will.

"Eat and let us celebrate our victory"

They devoured the meat and vegetables placed on the table as if they had not eaten in weeks. Ale was consumed and cups were filled over and over, each of them subjecting themselves to gluttony of epic proportions.

Framin sent out a call to Viyana, and the room filled with concubines of all shapes and sizes. Each of them carried ale, and along with it pipes of sweet smelling opiates. The room began to fill with the essence of evil and debauchery. He left them then, sure that they had returned to him in their entirety.

***

From the corner of his eye Bethrod saw Framin leave. He had moved himself furthest away from everyone, and had made it seem like he was imbibing of the pleasure provided by their lord. Each of his "brothers" had given themselves to the darkness encompassed in the room. Bethrod, however, had more important tasks on his mind. For years he had fooled his lord and his brothers. He had learned to hide his true self and send forth the vibrations needed to do so. He was smart—he had been smart hundreds of years ago, and in all that time he had increased his knowledge and his ability. Even during the "cleansing" ceremonies that Framin conducted he had been able to hide his essence and keep his learning growing.

In his experience even those that confessed themselves to be gods could be fooled, and his ambition, as far as he could tell, outstripped even this being. His brother Gouarong had long since fallen to Framin's power, but it wasn't so in the beginning.

46

Then he thought he might be able to influence their actions and alliances had been brokered. He had long since given up on that road though. They were weak and not as smart as him, and the hold that Framin had on them was too strong.

He sent out a trace smaller than an atom to follow Framin. He had done this numerous times, and from it had learned untold secrets and truths. But at this crucial stage he needed to learn everything he could. He knew that Framin was not a true being of this world, but was something else made up of the essence of the universe itself. He had watched as he decomposed his essence and mingled with that of the universe, and it was from that he had learned this trick. Up till now he had not been able to follow Framin to learn his true origin, but he was getting closer and that gave him hope. He still had time to learn more, and in that more he might discover the key that would give him the edge. So he let his trace go to call it and investigate it at a future time.

It was, he had to admit, an epic undertaking that Framin had orchestrated. He had managed over centuries to gain a foothold in every corner of the globe, and thus control tens of thousands of lives and vast resources. He had engineered his lattice of portals, each of them identical in construction and each of them designed to garner life's energies.

Bethrod looked round the room and at each of his "brothers," and though they were almost identical in appearance he could read their energy signatures and knew their differences. He decided he had had enough of the gathering, and leaving his human shell in the room he slipped his true essence out and away from the present. He needed time to think and time to plan. He went over in his mind what he knew of these "brothers."

Kahilja's city was in a cold land—his people were hardy,

warriors, horse riders that roamed the plains. Apart from the "City of Spires" there were very few other permanent settlements. They were nomads and set up camp where ever they decided to rest. The plains were interspersed with lakes of all sizes, some as big as seas and others no bigger than a herd of the cattle they drove along with them. The seasons were mainly harsh and cold, with a brief summer that allowed the plains to seed.

Handuris shared a continent, vast and way to the west, with Khaleber, Deelum, and Santarish. It had many climes, and ranged from desert to mangroves to fertile terraces. Their people were numerous, small industrious people who, encouraged by their lords, worshipped many gods of all shapes and sizes. Each of the gods, though, demanded sacrifices of livestock or humans.

Procarin ruled an area in a land that was green and lush, with rugged coastlines and soft rolling hills that were suited for the growing of grapes and olives. His people were scholars, but they also were fighters and fierce defenders of their lands. They relished the chance to discuss politics and alliances, and would defend these policies with their lives and armies. The country was ruled by a system of local, regional, and country wide governing bodies. Procarin had influence.

Akima, Itsuo, and Kaidi each controlled a province amongst a nation that was made up of divided islands linked by traders and an ability to navigate waters. The general populace was rigid and tradition bound. An overarching emperor controlled the nation, but he'd had to make alliances to control all the provinces, and as such each province could hold much sway. These three were plotting to destabilize and take the nation as a whole, and insert one of themselves as emperor.

48

Faisal and Bakir were tribal leaders of desert people in the hot dry land way to the north of Mehem. This land was ruled by Bremen, who was seen as a god made flesh, so the two were and had to be capable of conducting their business and schemes below his sight. They were sorely tested at all times.

Bethrod himself held lands that were inhabited by a people that were raiders. They were a fierce, tall people that liked nothing better than a chance to sack and conquer new lands. Tribal in nature, they too were nomadic till they conquered a people. Then they put down roots, set up a ruler, and set about building new empires. They were at the same time bent on creating a peaceful empire. All their conquering was done in the name of coalescing disparate people and tribes into a mighty nation.

Framin did not see this, as the killing, looting, and conquering suited his need. Bethrod had been careful to balance the greed in his people's nature, and also fill them with the desire to sit at peace with each other. His nature, which was hidden, was to build something that benefited the whole. He needed to be sure, however, that his reach increased. He knew there would be a day of reckoning with Framin and his brothers, and he gathered his resources against that day.

Was it enough? He wasn't sure, but alongside the power and vision that Framin had given him, he also heard another, a promise of eternal peace and joy, and he longed for that more. He had taken a long time to work out where this desire came from, and it tugged at him from time to time and appealed to his essence. What he did know was that things were gathering. The time for different alliances and plans was coming. He just didn't know yet where these were or where they would come from, though he had forged some alliances. He was happy to ride each of these waves of thought and possibilities and see where they led. He knew there was more, much more than Framin had promised.

He felt Framin return to the room, and with him came the trail he had sent. He gathered it in and would look later at what he knew. He returned to his earthly body and became alert.

"Brothers," came Framin's voice. "It is time to return and carry on with the plans we have taken so long to put in place. Things are moving now, and the universal lines are beginning to converge. Soon there will be a reckoning, and we need be ready. We will have a chance to become what we know we deserve and desire. Make ready your plans. I will visit each of you, and you can show me what you have accomplished."

***

Framin again began his haunting chant, and his Gouarong began to fade. As the last one disappeared from his view he pushed a line of power that followed them all, and he sat to test his link.

CHAPTER 8
ICHANCHA

Ichancha sat atop the rock and was at peace. Her energies ebbed and flowed to and from her center, and she relished the feeling. It was cold on top of the mountain—remnants of snow lay around in small pockets blown by the wind against rock and into small hollows, but she hadn't felt it. She had tuned into the universal energies and had watched the goings on of Framin and his Gouarong. Some years earlier she had discovered this ripple in the earth's energies and had tuned in to watch what was happening, and she had continued to do so for many years now.

She didn't understand what was happening and how it was happening, but she knew that there was something evil occurring, and she knew it was of importance. So she watched when she could, and she waited.

Deep in her mind she almost remembered something about herself—it was close, very close indeed. A few decades ago she had just seemed to find herself here, with no recollection of how or why it had happened. She waited for the day that someone would call to her. She knew it would come, but she didn't know from where or by whom. Until that point she was prepared to wait, to watch, and to learn....

Chapter 9
Bremen

Saloora followed Elgred through the narrow streets, not noticing the hustle and bustle increasing as they went. They arrived at an open square with multiple fountains and edged with eateries of all kinds. The sound of the running water soothed her, and indeed since she had been with Elgred the city did not seem so foreboding at all, and exuded a certain harmony. As she looked around she could see many smiling faces. There didn't seem to be much dirt or rubbish or any people begging, or even any people poorly dressed.

The fountains were adorned with flowers and plants that added to the friendly ambience of the square. Fruit trees bearing dates, oranges, and a variety of persimmon were dotted around, and people took their leisure seated on the many small terraced areas or standing around carts that were selling food and drink.

Here and there people were singing and playing instruments while others were holding forth on miracles, and lauding benefits provided by Bremen. Everywhere she looked prosperity and calm was the main feature. Saloora was, however, honed and trained to notice detail, and she saw here and there a person that seemed at odds with the surroundings, acting as hard as they could as if nothing were wrong. But they had a tension that she could not miss.

She touched Elgred's arm and spoke to him. "Is there some kind of tension in the city? It's just that I notice the odd person who seems to be a little out of place and trying too hard to act normally."

Elgred laughed. "Yes, you do well to spot them. There is a faction in the city that no matter how hard we try we can't seem to eliminate entirely. They are followers of Framin. They come here to spy and report to him on what is happening. We try and corner them when we can and teach them the way that leads to light and hope, but Framin's training is deeply ingrained and we do not get through to many. Those that we can't persuade we send back to him."

"You don't imprison them? Or kill them?" she asked.

"No, we do not. It's against our nature to do such things. We cannot teach and talk about peace and the benefits of collaboration if we either kill or lock people up." Elgred smiled at her.

"I have found," she said, "that there are times that you have to fight for your own survival, though killing for the sake of it is something that is against my nature."

He looked at her again as if weighing up what to say next, but opted instead to say, "Not too far now—just across the square and one more street. Once we are there we will have time to discuss much of these things, and you will see what we have planned. You will have no small part to play in this venture, and I suspect your nature will serve you well in the near future."

They came to the end of the square and moved up a short street, and there in front of them was a building the likes of which Saloora had never seen. It was not vast and magnificent as she'd expected; in fact, it was quite humble in size. It did, though, draw her toward it as though it were inviting her in, promising her rest and peace and happiness. It was a low-slung building, much wider than it was tall, and had a wide terrace that stretched the whole front of the building. Around the terrace were many seats and partitioned areas, split from others by rambling vines that created natural partitions.

The stairs up to the terrace were made of some kind of huge polished limestone, and she wondered how they even moved them.

The building itself was also made from the stones, and it had what could only be described as low parapets along the front, each of them adorned with colored glass that sparkled. Just beyond the parapets she could see what appeared to be a giant upside-down ball.

Many people sat around on the terrace, all talking and just enjoying the chance to pass the time of day with each other. There did not seem to be any guards, and as they approached the building no one seemed to either notice or care that they were heading for the opening. They crossed the terrace and headed toward a pair of oak doors, plain to look at but none the less thick and sturdy, with ornate carvings and brass studs on each door.

As they passed the threshold Saloora felt the hairs on her arms and neck stand up — not in a fashion that related to danger, just as if someone had blown a gentle breeze across her skin. She stopped and looked back.

"Now you know why we need no guards here," Elgred

said. "No one may enter who has any malice in them. I would say that right now we are in one of the safest places I know."

She turned back, and they continued to walk. The air inside was cool yet warm enough. Light poured in through the terrace, and the colored windows cast shades and shapes in every direction. It held an almost mystical quietness that seeped into the body, spreading a further feeling of belonging.

There was little to show any opulence, and the décor was modest, functional, and yet beautiful at the same time. No showing of wealth with gold or jewels, just décor that made her feel at home and welcome. An earthy quality about the whole place held a suggestion that it was a part of something much more grand; everything had a connection to everything else, and each had its place and purpose.

They walked towards a wall that was covered with arched entrances, almost portal like in their appearance, each one there to entice you to discover what lay beyond. Elgred steered them to an opening in the center, and they passed through into a circular room. Books and manuscripts covered all of the walls and stretched well up to the vaulted circular ceiling. Several balconies ran around the room, almost as if in concentric circles that led her eyes up to the center of the ceiling, which was spectacular in that it opened to the heavens. She could see stars and planets and moons, and lines connecting them in all directions. It was mesmerizing.

Towards the back of the room and seated around a wooden desk were two people. Saloora stopped then.

In front of her was the most beautiful woman she had ever seen. She stood, clothed in shifts of cloth that were almost transparent and floated around her, leaving everything yet nothing to the imagination. Her body was lithe yet seductive in its roundness, her legs slim and long yet muscular in nature. Her hair was raven and fell across her shoulders and down her back, opulent in its richness. Her face was breathtaking in its beauty, with a bone structure that showed off every angle and feature, all of which complimented the other.

She turned her gaze on Saloora, and in an instant Saloora knew here was a woman that knew her soul, and indeed the reason for her very existence. It was disquieting yet soothing at the same time.

Next to the woman was a young man, much the same age as Saloora, broad shouldered yet not too tall. His head was covered in unruly straw gold hair that fit his face. Square jawed and strong featured, his eyes held a kindness and understanding well beyond his years.

Saloora felt a tug unlike anything she had felt before, an almost primal urge to touch this man and for him to touch her. She was unsure of her next step.

That spell was broken when the woman, who identified herself as Charina, spoke. "Come Saloora, come and meet Bremen." She smiled as she spoke. "Let us get to know each other and talk of the future. There will be time for your urges in the future. I can tell you, though, that they were meant to be. They come as no surprise to anyone here other than you, and I suspect Bremen himself." She laughed…it was clear, strong, and sang out to them all. It even tasted of joy.

"Don't tease them so, Charina," Elgred said. "I thought we had agreed that we would talk of this as things progressed."

"It's clear to me that there won't need to be much talking for these two to know that they are each half of the other—they have already felt it. It is written on their faces."

The joy it brought her was again infectious, and they all

stood facing each other and smiling with what could only be described as a meeting of long time lovers, those that understood each other deeply, those whose souls had travelled together across eternity — there would be no secrets here.

***

Bremen was stunned. Charina had told him Elgred was bringing someone to meet him, but he was unprepared for the reaction he had the moment he saw Saloora. At first he thought that Elgred had brought with him a lioness, but that was nonsense — she was walking on two legs, though her hair was golden like a lioness's coat. She flowed as she walked, exuding a prowess that was both regal and dangerous. Her eyes were also golden, and glinted as she looked around. He'd thought that Charina was the most beautiful women he had ever seen, but he was wrong; here she stood before him now. He felt a tug and wanted to gather her up, but he stood fast.

"Bremen, meet Saloora, or Ahhbreshemen as her people call her. Saloora, meet Bremen."

Elgred and Charina backed away and left them both standing, watching each other.

Saloora spoke first. "I don't like and have never liked the use of Ahhbreshemen, so Saloora will do." She reached towards him with her left hand. He took her hand and ran his hand up her arm, and they pulled together closer till they were almost entangled with each other

"I am Bremen, Saloora, and I give myself to you completely. All essence that I have is yours to take and share, and do with as you please." He leant in even closer and kissed her softly.

"Your essence I take," she said, pulling away. "And in return I give you that which you will take from me."

Bremen untangled himself and took her by the hand, and

moved them both towards an opening leading to a balcony that overlooked a large courtyard in the center of the building. It was beautiful, and filled with flowers and plants and a running stream. He held her again then, and began to speak.

"It seems like I have waited for you all my short life, but I didn't know that I was doing it. I have a feeling that somehow you have completed me, and now I seem to be more at peace. I feel the need to tell you about myself.

"I have lived here all my life. My father was Bremen before me, and Elgred showed him ways to try and reconcile our people, He made great strides and the city has become a place of safety, of learning, and of the telling of tales that will make the world understand the benefit of the things we do.

"Since I was a small child I have been talking to people of how to become one with the energies of the world, how it benefits them, and how kindness, compassion, forgiveness, and most of all love can overcome everything. Until this point, though, I hadn't realized that there was a different depth to love, love that could be kept only for two, not shared amongst everyone. I have learned today, just now on meeting you, that even more than I imagined may be possible, this love I feel right now can be used to show even greater things to everyone. Elgred talked to me about the need to feed your own soul with love and then share it. I thought I had that in the love of the people, but now I know I was limiting myself in that knowledge.

"I have much that I want to share with you, much that I would like to tell you and show you. Will you let me? Will you let me share what I know? Will you share with me what you know, and we can build something amazing, something wonderful for everyone?"

"I will gladly let you share everything with me," she said.

"And in return I will share my story with you. I am not sure what this is, but I am sure it is the beginning of something. The beginning of something that I need."

CHAPTER 10
THE ROAD TO MEHEM.

Dregar returned them to the "now," and Elji startled at the change.

"You will have to get used to that," Dregar said. "Let's go and visit your mother and brothers; you should say your goodbyes. It is unlikely that you will see them again for some time, and while it might be prudent to just sneak away, I don't relish the thought that your mother will worry, and I have no desire to cause any undue pain and suffering. We will tell her that I am a rich merchant from the city and that I need an apprentice. I know that she loves you, but we will sweeten the deal with gold. Enough gold that she need worry no more. It will ease the loss, though as a mother there is never a good time to let your children go. If she is unconvinced we can go to the inn and Jeelan will tell her what he knows of me, and I can ease the burden of your leaving and the discussion around it with a little manipulation of the essence around her. She will be worried, yet willing by the time we have finished. Also, I think you have some goodbyes to say to your young lady friend at the inn—no doubt she will miss your attention."

They walked down the path to his house and entered through the door. Abriana and the boys, when they saw Elji was not alone, bolted upright.

"It's OK, it's OK; he is a friend," Elji offered.

Still the brothers looked uneasy and reached for clubs that were leaning against the large fireplace.

Dregar spoke. "I am Dregar, a merchant from the city of Mehem. I think you will have seen me from time to time staying at the inn?" His voice had a quality that soothed them, and they settled a little more. "Elji and I have spoken over many years, and I come to ask something of you. I am looking for an apprentice to help me run my trade between the cities, and I would like to take Elji with me and teach him of commerce. We have spoken about it at different times, and I have told him of cities and lands other than where you now live. It is possible that some of his stories may have been influenced by those tales." He smiled at them. "He will be gone for a long time, but his future will be bright, and it will be the making of him."

Elji decided he would lend some weight to the story. "It's OK, Mum. This is something I have dreamed of, and Dregar and I have spoken many times, as he says. You know I am restless and I dream of adventure. I need to be doing something with my life other than working in the quarry. The village sees me as someone different to everyone else; it will not come as a surprise that I leave the village. Dregar and I have spoken, and we have agreed that he will pay you ten years' worth of partial wages to ease my leaving and help you with the future. I will also be able to send money to you, and I can come visit from time to time when I am travelling." He looked at her, then at his brothers.

Abriana and the boys began to look at each other—puzzlement and an air of distrust still held the air.

"I know this all seems a little sudden, and you will have lots of questions," said Dregar. "Why don't we go to the inn? I will buy you all food, and we can talk about this. It would do you no harm to listen, and at worst you will have eaten." He smiled again. "What do you say? If no one else is, I am certainly hungry, and could do with some food. And a good flagon of fine ale never comes amiss!"

Elji walked towards his mum and put his arm around her waist. "Come on, Mum, let's go and talk. Dregar has much to teach me, and I am more than willing to learn. Who knows, I may even get to see one of the beasts I talk to you about." The smile on Elji's face relaxed his mother, and the boys began to let down their guard.

"You know," said Caldrian, the most voluble of the brothers, "that there are no beasts that you talk of, and if your going away at least stops you from talking about them and us from listening to your tales, then something good will have come." He laughed. "Though I don't know who we will tease once you are gone, and who will do all the fetching and carrying." All the brothers smiled at that.

They all stood and began to move to the door, the ice broken. The teasing starting again as they made their way out of the house. Abriana, however, stayed close to her youngest son, and seemed to want the comfort of him being near her.

The inn was, as usual, fairly busy, and they made their way to a table. They ordered food and began to talk. Dregar had a way with words, though Elji suspected he was manipulating something as he had said he would do. The mood lightened as they ate and drank, and as Dregar expanded on the benefits of Elji taking on an apprenticeship. By the time they had finished they were all talking with great excitement about the opportunity and possibilities that it would lead to.

"When will you leave?" Abriana asked.

"In the morning," said Dregar. "We need to be away early. There is quite a way to go, and I have neglected my business in Mehem a little longer than I wanted. We will take the main highway, and with luck we will get passage with a passing tradesman of some kind to help speed up the journey."

"The morning? So soon?" She started to worry again, but thinking on it she realized there was no good or bad time to let one of your sons go. "Let's go home and pack what you need. I can give some food for the road, and we can talk while I do it."

"Before we go I would just like to find Ingria and tell her that I am leaving. I will be along soon," Elji said, and he smiled and got up from the table to go and find her.

Elji found Ingria where he always found her at this time of day. Just as the sun was setting each day she would wait for him, sitting on the edge of the well that served the inn, staring at the night sky with his dog at her feet, content and fast asleep.

He looked at her as he walked up, trying to work out what he was about to tell her. Of all the people in the village she was the one that he would miss most. They had been friends since they were small children, and Ingria had never teased him but had listened to his stories and dreams, and even joined in them, relishing his enthusiasm.

She turned and saw him and smiled. "Elji," she said. "There you are. I thought for a moment you weren't coming to see me." She smiled again.

"Now Ingria, have I not come to see you every time I have said I would? I wouldn't just not turn up. Even if I did, I think you would come and search for me, wouldn't you?"

"Yes, yes I would."

Elji felt uncomfortable about what he was about to tell her. He felt like he was about to commit some kind of betrayal, and it must have shown on his face.

"Oh! What's wrong, Elji? Anyone would think you had come to say goodbye to me for good. Your face looks so sad." She stopped what she was saying and looked at him again.

"What's wrong, Elji? What has happened?"

He sighed and sat down next to her. "Remember how we talk about great adventures and all the things I would like to see, and how there is a much bigger world than just the village, and how amazing it would be to see some of that? Remember how we said that someday you and I would leave the village and make our fortune, and see some of those things together? Well, something has happened that means I can do those things, but I have to do them now and I have to do them on my own."

He dropped his head and looked at his hands as if he could find the words he needed next somewhere in them. She reached out and took his hand gently and looked at him.

"Elji, those were children's promises to each other. They were dreams, beautiful dreams, and ones we would have been happy with. But we both have known that there was little chance of them coming true. We know that my place is here. You never had any ambition to be an innkeeper." She smiled at him. "And if I am honest, I never had any ambition to leave my home behind."

They both fell silent.

"Ingria," he said. "You always were the more practical one, always going along with my dreams and stories, always laughing with me, always being my friend. I will miss you the

65

most. Will you look after Aker for me?"

He could see that despite her bravado her eyes were filling with tears. He put his arm around her shoulder and pulled her in closer. "I will miss you, you know? You have been a true friend."

He stood to leave and she stood with him, but she took his hand and led him towards the hay barn at the back of the inn. She needed to let him know how she felt about him.

***

Dregar and Elji had been walking down the highway for three days. All the while Dregar had been talking to Elji of the nature of things and how they worked. The boy had been astounded at the connections between life, and indeed all things. The concept that he had most struggled with was the one in which all things were possible, and were a reality in some other possible present, and the future was what you made it. Dregar had told him that all things came from you, and you controlled what your experience of reality was.

He had explained it like this.

"All things come from you. There is nothing that is real unless you allow it to be. Of course, things do happen that you have no control over, and this is because there are millions of others utilizing the energy to create their own reality. But how you deal with them and what you make of them determines the outcome. Let me ask you a question. When you look around and see a tree, where do you see it?"

Elji pointed to the trees. "Over there," he said.

"No, you are wrong," said Dregar. "You see them inside of you, as you see all things inside you. Your eyes take in the light that is around you, and they project an image onto the back of your eye and your mind sees the image there. Now I know

66

that is simplistic, but do you understand that? That means that nothing exists outside of you, and without you allowing it to do so. If you chose not to see the trees they are not there. All of that is controlled by you.

"Those beings that have a firm hold on this concept are the ones that can influence most of those around them and get them to believe what they want. It is through this that control is gained. Once you understand that it is your manipulation of the energies that creates the present, then you can start to put forward your version of the 'Now,' and in doing that you gain control and can imagine anything you want."

Elji had struggled with this concept right from the start. How could it be that he decided what happened? He just didn't understand it, and Dregar had explained the same concept a number of different ways.

"How you think about things directly impacts what the reality is…let me try and explain it to you this way." He gathered his thoughts. "I know of all things so far that you miss your dog. I want you to think about him for a moment. Do you remember the times you were trying to do your chores, and he would be around dragging stuff off that you needed and being a nuisance? You know, like taking the turnips you were giving to the pigs, and causing you more work chasing him and retrieving them? Do you remember how annoying that was and how you felt? But then I want you to think about other times, times you were happy and smiling and he would do the same thing. But these times you would laugh at him and chase him, and you were happy and content and it was a game. What was the difference between these two things? It was you; it was the way you wanted to see the situation. Does that make any more sense? Because what you have done is created your own reality depending on how you chose to feel."

Elji thought. Of course…how could it be that simple? Of course those things were the same, but he felt differently about each at certain times, and it was obvious that it was because of how he felt. WOW! *So I can feel what I want about anything, and that will change how I see it*. It was a shift in thinking, that was for sure.

"Of course, it isn't quite as straight forward as that. As I have told you before, all things are energy, and if someone else is manipulating the same energy it can be a conflict. The one that has the greatest belief changes that outcome, but put quite simply, what I have explained to you is the basic concept of everything."

Elji thought for a moment. "So if someone hits me with a stick, are you saying that is not real?"

"Now that is a perfect question, and it relates to the reality of all things. Of course here in this plane and at this time everything is real, because as a consciousness we all believe in the same reality; as a collective we believe that things hurt us, and as a collective we believe that we can die or starve or become ill. These are concepts that humanity has accepted as realities. This touches on much of what we are trying to achieve here. When we reach Mehem I am going to introduce you to some people, and they are going to explain to you what we need to do and why we need to do it."

Elji fell silent. So many things were almost in the grasp of his understanding, and yet not. He sighed, yet he felt that he had gained a lot from these discussions with Dregar and he wanted to understand more.

"Just up ahead," said Dregar, "is a path that leads to a place I think we should visit on our way to Mehem. In any case the rest will do us some good, and I am sure we have the time. Yes, yes, we have time."

CHAPTER 11
THE HAROOD

They turned off onto the path and soon were walking through light woods in a slight upward direction. As they walked the path got more and more narrow and the vegetation thicker, making its way onto the path. Elji thought that soon it would become impassable. He was beginning to wonder if Dregar had taken them down the wrong path altogether. He did seem unconcerned, though, and Elji just continued to follow him. They walked for some time, indeed what seemed like hours, and just as he thought they could go no further, the path opened up and Elji could hear running water. The air also cleared, and had a crisp, healthy feel about it.

Dregar kept walking and they came to the edge of what appeared to be a very large pond—not quite a lake, but big enough that they would need some kind of boat to cross it. Elji could see that in the middle there was a small island, and off to the left a waterfall that was causing the sound that Elji had heard.

Dregar stopped and crouched down near the edge of the

pond like he was waiting.

"Are we there?" asked Elji.

"Yes."

"I don't see anything other than the lake."

"Let's wait a while. And when I say a while, I mean that it may be some time. You may as well sit."

Elji sat and got himself into some kind of comfortable position. "What are we waiting for?"

"You will see. Just be patient and hold your inquisitive questioning. I am going to get some rest." At that Dregar laid himself on the grass edge of the large pond and closed his eyes.

Elji had no choice but to choose to wait, and so he did. As he waited his mind began to drift, and in it he began to see visions of lines and specs much like he had seen when he had looked closely at the galrass. They were pulsating and moving, and he began to see visions of beings walking along the lines towards him. They were human like in form, and even at the distance they were from them he could tell that they were smaller than anyone he had ever met. They shone with a light that came from within them and radiated out towards him. They were coming closer and closer. He started awake.

Strange, he thought, and wondered if the galrass was trying to show him something. He was about to take it from his pocket when Dregar said "Your stone won't work here—it is not needed. Let's go." And he stood.

He hadn't noticed, but between where they had rested and the island there was a small yet undeniable path. Dregar set off. As they walked the path dissolved behind them, leaving only the water, and he began to wonder how they might get back. He was not a keen swimmer, though he had played in the local stream often enough at home, so if he needed to he could.

71

Reaching the island, they stepped off the bridge-like path and it disappeared altogether. In front of them was a staircase that wound down into the earth. From the opening was coming the sound of music, and a smell that reminded him that he was hungry. Dregar headed down and Elji followed.

As they reached the bottom they came face to face with one of the beings that Elji had seen while waiting at the edge of the pond. She—he assumed it was a she—was no bigger than three feet tall, and was made from a glow much like the essence strands he had seen in the galrass. She floated rather than walked, though she did have legs and was human in appearance.

Welcome, came a voice inside his head. *It has been a very long time since Dregar has brought anyone to see us.* With that she looked at him, and Elji got the feeling she was deciding if she was happy he was there. *We are the Harood, and you can call me Jemba,* she said as she swept her hand around, indicating the others that were nearby. Each of them was engrossed in a song; it was both haunting and beautiful, tonal and almost tangible in its sound. They all grasped what looked like a tether of light that stretched into a central dome and disappeared. *Of course, even though he hadn't told us you were coming, we knew you were here. After all, it is our nature to watch all. Come,* Jemba said. *Now that you are here in person, Koth will want to meet you.* She turned and moved away. They both followed.

Koth was standing at what appeared to be the edge of where they were gathered. Beyond him was nothing other than a deep crystal grey intertwined with lines. As they neared him the habitat they were in expanded to accommodate the fact that they were walking towards it, and a much more familiar earthy setting of a continuation of a glade emerged.

"Dregar!" he said. "Welcome. And this must be Elji?"

Elji had long since ceased to be amazed at what appeared to be impossible things, and he just bowed his head a little, as it seemed like an appropriate thing to do.

Koth looked at him and Elji returned the favor, noticing that he was a male though he was made of the same stuff and was the same size as Jemba. The difference being he exuded an energy that he could feel rather than see. It filled Elji with a sense of insignificance so real that it almost knocked him to his knees.

"My apologies," said Koth. "Let me take care of that." He flicked his hand and the feeling left, and there before him was a being of legend that Elji had seen many times in his dreams. A warrior of such fierceness, and yet a beauty that was impossible not to be drawn towards. The being began to move towards him, and Elji felt a hopelessness so complete he was sure he was going to die. "Perhaps this suits your imagination better?" Boomed the being.

"Koth!" said Jemba. "There is no need to frighten the life out of the boy. He doesn't need to see the things of his dreams turn to reality, or for those things to threaten him."

The being disappeared and Koth returned in his place. "You are right." He smiled. "Though it is still an important lesson to be had; not everything is as it seems to be, and this may keep the boy alive in the near future. He is going to meet those that will beguile, confuse, and want to kill him, and he needs be ready for the task."

Elji looked around him and caught the eye of Dregar. "Things that may want to kill me" he said, his voice somewhat higher in tone than normal. "What is he talking about? I didn't know that we would be facing danger in any of this. I didn't know my life may be at risk!"

"Did you think," said Dregar, "that we could just ignore all that has happened to you and not include you in the struggle we make on a daily basis? As I told you, we are going to Mehem, and when we get there we will speak with people that ensure this world is safe. But it is important that you understand the dangers as well as the beauty that you will see. It is also really important that we make alliances where we can with those that can help us to overcome the things that Koth speaks about.

"The minute you found the galrass and nearly died, you were catapulted into the future custody of this world whether you wished it or not. The essence of the universe doesn't do these things without good reason, and something has been seen in you that we hope may help to tip the balance in our favor. None of us, as yet, knows what that might be, but each of us will have a role to play

"The Harood that you see before you are beings of the universe and not of this planet. That we see them here is just a construct to make dealing with them easier than it might be. There are things afoot here that we must deal with. We have to plan carefully what we do, because our influence will have a direct impact on the future of the world. Listen to what Koth tells you of the nature of things—some of it I have told you already."

Koth created comfortable chairs from the essence around him and they all sat. He began his tale.

***

"There was no beginning of everything as far back as anyone who is of the essence of the universe, or who creates the essence, can recall. As far as we all know we have been here forever, and there were others before us that were here forever themselves. Though that may sound confusing, it is the nature of the universe. Time, as you know it, does not exists other than that which we create artificially to frame existence.

"The four original creators of the essence, we assume, are Elgred, Charina, Lhapso, and Ichancha, and they still remain. Perhaps they were the all in the first place. Of that no entity is sure. If they themselves know then they do not tell, and the essence itself holds no trace of any truth of it.

"In this timeline Ichancha has been lost for millennia, and we can find no trace of her true force, though recently there has been found a possibility that she endures still as the faintest form of her true self. There is still hope that we may discover her, and she may yet have a part to play. We will have to wait and see.

"The Four were the creators of all things. They come from the essence itself, and they were able to use that essence to create more. In the beginning they were content to create worlds and suns and moons. All of this was done by combined will and desire. Where the desire came from they do not understand—just that it was, and we do not question. Time elapsed, as you know it, and they began to create life on the planets. Some were simple forms and self-sustaining, but others were much more complex. The aim, as they tell it, was to create forces that could join them in the manipulation and creation.

"Life forms were born with the ultimate aim of progressing each to the understanding of the simplicity of the universe, and how all things are from one. They discovered, however, that many life forms were not suited. Some worlds died and were forgotten, but a few flourished, and over time were able to evolve to the point that they could join The Four at a certain level.

"The first of these races was from a planet called Voldara. These life forces seemed to have the ability to accept the understanding and were quick to adapt, and evolved to become the first to join The Four. They were taught and given incredible understanding, with the ability to influence and create life with the aim to incorporate more into the creators. Of this race only one now survives—his name is Framin. He was the greatest of them, and had an unquenchable need to create. Because of his desire to attain more, he realized that he could utilize the life forces he and The Four created to enhance his ability and understanding. He became consumed with this task, and created life just for the sake of destruction. Elgred could not allow this use of the essence; he stripped Framin of his ability, and in your terms he cast him down, placing him on a planet he had created in the hope that he might reconsider his ambition and return to the true calling of creation.

"Framin did not do this. He hid himself away, learning to hide his essence, and plotted to regain all his understanding and ability. He moved from world to world, causing destruction and death and striving to regain that which he'd lost. He plots still to this day, and his need is great. He desires to return to The Four, but as an equal.

"The Four have watched him over eons. Every time they created a new life force, Framin would try and turn them to his way, corrupt the energies, sing the song of the dark and promise much, draining their energy as he could. In the beginning it was easy to control him and limit his damage, and turn these life forces to the growing of the essence. But Framin was still able to influence enough that not all life forces evolved to be part of The One. Even today they strive to control him, and the latest test is here on this planet.

76

"We, the Harood, came from a planet within a different galaxy many eons ago, and we were tasked with watching each planet and the life force, and warning of Framin's plans. We hold the universal lines of every living thing on each planet, and we watch and influence where we can in an effort to align the beings of planets to be part of the all. We have become that which you see now.

"Many other races have joined the collective consciousness of the essence that which we call The One, and together we all monitor the universe to keep it aligned and allow for further creation. As a collective we have agreed on the level of intervention allowed to give direction to a life force to become part of The One, and we follow the plan and rules diligently.

"This planet seems to have evolved a life force like no other in its capacity for understanding and love, but at the same time has the capacity to hate and destroy like no other we have seen so far. This is why Framin tries to influence here, and together we must not let him succeed.

"What we all strive to achieve is to become harmonious with all things everywhere, whatever their nature. But we must let things progress without direct intervention so that we never face the difficulty again that has occurred with Framin, allowing those with darker desires to try and gain things for themselves. The true nature of everything is that while there is light there is also dark, or good and evil in your terms, and until we can banish the dark forever, we must be ever vigilant.

"Of course, this is not everything I could tell you of the making of what we see today and where we are, but we would be sitting here for eons to give that telling justice."

Koth's eyes narrowed, and he was looking at Elji as if weighing something up.

"You will find that as you adapt and learn of the essence, all things are possible. It is yet to be seen whether your choosing has been one we can rejoice in or regret. We hope it is the first and you can grow to your true potential. It will not be easy, and you will be tempted by many things. But if you are willing, the future you can create could be the most wonderful thing you can imagine.

"We will talk more on these things as our paths cross again. One thing I will give you to try and help you on your journey is that when you can truly give without expectation or need for recognition, you will have learned that thing which is most important; you will have learned who you are."

***

A silence fell around them as they each absorbed what Koth had said.

"I think," said Dregar, "that you may have digested as much as can be expected in a short time, and talking anymore around these things may just confuse you. With all we have seen it will be better that we skip a little of the journey on foot and move ourselves closer to Mehem. This will let you think about what Koth has told you, and what you have seen."

Dregar removed his stick from his pack and manipulated it in an intricate pattern, and he and Elji were transported to outside the city; still quite some distance away, but they were almost there. Dregar led them down the road and towards the outer edges of the city. Elji could hear and feel the energy of the place. There were more people than he had ever seen in his life.

They entered the city of Mehem.

Chapter 12
The gathering

The city was bustling; people were walking everywhere, and there were hawkers and sellers of all kinds plying their trade, from sweet cakes to clothing. Elji was fascinated. Dregar led him through streets that twisted and turned, until at last they came to an opening with a large low-slung building at one end. They headed that way.

As they entered through the opening they were greeted by a man, small in stature but as wide as he was small. He reached out his hand and said "Dregar, it's so good to see you again. It's been a long time."

Dregar took the hand and they shook firmly, pulling each other in and embracing as old friends do.

"Elji," said Dregar. "This is Jawarat. He is the keeper and organizer of this place, and more like the keeper and organizer of everyone who enters it. Nothing comes, goes, or happens here that he does not know about, and he manages it all with patience and grace that no man should be endowed with. Except, of course, when things start to go wrong; then he has

79

the attitude of a baited bear." Dregar laughed, and Jawarat laughed along with him.

"Welcome, Elji, and good to meet you. Are you staying long" Jawarat asked Dregar.

"I'm not sure. We need to see Elgred and find out what must be done, and I have news for him that may be of some importance. Is he here?"

"Yes, he's here. You are not the only ones who have come to visit in the last few days. We have someone unexpected, but waited for, and she has caused quite a stir. Not least of all to Bremen, who seems to have grown so close to her you would imagine they had known each other all their lives, though of course they are strangers. If you ask me she has changed him, and he has become a man in a matter of days. I guess you must be tired. Let me show you where you can stay, and I will go and tell Elgred you are here and find out what must be done. I will send someone with a message once I know what's what."

Elji and Dregar were led down a long side corridor and given rooms separate but connected. Each looked out inwards towards a central quadrangle, though it was like nothing Elji had ever seen before. It was encased in something, and when he looked up it showed a vision of planets and stars, millions and millions of them, though outside he knew it was daylight. On the ground was vegetation of all kinds, and a stream. It was peaceful in the extreme, and felt like there was nothing beyond it.

As Elji looked he thought he caught a slight whisper of a song so faint and distant it was almost imperceptible, yet it seemed to call to him and give him hope. He was fascinated. He turned and looked around the room. It was comfortable, with everything he needed, and functional, with no unnecessary decorations or shows of riches, though it felt like it fit him.

He was tired. The last few days had been confusing, surprising, and taxing. What he had learned and seen had drawn all energy from him. He needed sleep, and thought it would be OK to lie down for a bit and get some rest. He was sure someone would get him if he was needed.

***

Dregar sat on the edge of his bed and waited. He could have sent a thought out to Elgred, but would let Jawarat do his duty. Some of the comments Jawarat had made had intrigued him, and he was interested to find out what was going on. As was his way, he didn't like to extend his mind and use the essence to gather information in places he considered were friendly; he preferred the human form of communication in these instances. Most of the times on his travels he was constantly checking what was going on, and while it was not tiring but natural to take information this way, he did like the surprise he got when he had the opportunity to use human communication. All his kind had learned to close off themselves when they needed to — it was a unique gift they had.

There was a knock and he opened the door. The messenger bid him come outside and follow him. "We will get your friend," he said.

"No, let him rest," said Dregar. "There is time for him to learn what he must after that."

The messenger led him to where the others waited. Elgred, Charina, Bremen, and Saloora were seated around a low table. They were deep in conversation, but rose when they saw him.

"Hello, my friend," said Elgred as he came to embrace him, closely followed by Charina. Bremen also nodded his greeting, and was indeed pleased to see him.

81

"Hello, Dregar," said Saloora. "It is good to see you again."

"Ahh, now I see the meaning of Jawarat's words." He laughed his short laugh and smiled. "I did not know you were here, Saloora, but I am pleased to see that you found your way. It seems that things are moving along apace. I too have someone you must all meet, but he is resting. He has taken on a lot of information and understanding in the last few days, and I suspect it will be overwhelming for him. I did think at one time of reaching out to you, Elgred, but thought that you would know what was happening, and decided if you hadn't reached out for me there was no urgency."

"You talk of Elji, and of his finding and using the galrass?" Elgred asked.

"Yes," said Dregar. "It seems he was able somehow to find one, and what is even more important, use it, the doing of which nearly killed him. I assume that you had something to do with that?"

"No, it was as much of a surprise to me as to you," said Elgred. "I too felt it. There are things even now that amaze me. I thought that every galrass was under the control of those we know, and the rest were guarded by the Kuwali. It worries me that there are occurrences that we know nothing of. There was a time that such things would never have escaped any of us, so it is either that we are too consumed by the current undertaking, or that there is something at work that needs some investigation. If it is the latter, then that could also mean that something is able to hide from those that are watching the universal essence lines, or one of them is compromised in some way. I don't feel that anyone is hiding anything from us, but that doesn't mean it is not so. It is something of major concern, and something we need to spend some time understanding."

"I stopped on the way here to talk to the Harood," said Dregar. "They didn't tell me that anything was amiss, so I can only assume, as you say, that there is something deeper at work. I am sure that, though you are focused on the current time and situation, you would know of all eventualities. You have nurtured the birth and beginning of many civilizations before, and we have never had such an occurrence."

"Only once in everything that we remember has such a thing happened," said Charina, "and it was at the time we lost Ichancha. I wonder where she is now? Perhaps the time has come to find her, in case in her current state she is managing to confuse the essence somehow. It does seem that things are starting to coalesce, such as the fact that Ahhbreshemen is here, though she doesn't know yet of her status in all this." Charina looked at Saloora. "We are yet to enlighten her and Bremen of their part in all of this."

Saloora looked at them all. "You use my name given by the tribe as though it is known and has importance in what is happening. Is there something I should know?"

"Yes, most definitely there is," said Charina. "I don't think we can say what your part is going to be yet. I think we will wait till Elji joins us, and explore the possibilities together. I suspect that if Dregar and he have visited the Harood, there are things he can tell that would surprise you."

"In the meantime," said Elgred, "let's enjoy the fact that we are all here, and let the troubles of everything slide by for a while. There will be plenty of time for us to be embroiled in things that will be difficult in the undertaking."

***

Elji woke and took a moment to remember where he was. It had become dark, and he noticed that candles had been lit

83

in his room. He must have been more tired than he thought to have slept so long. He sat up and swung his legs over the edge of the bed. He was surprised that no one had come to wake him as had been said. Still, not to worry too much. He was sure that had he been needed he would indeed have been woken by someone.

He stood and made his way to the large windows. As he did he passed the table and noticed fruit had been placed there, along with water. He took some of both and stood staring out the window.

He heard a knock on the door and turned and made his way over to see who it was. The man who had showed them the room was standing outside.

"They are waiting for you. Would you like to follow me?"

Elji placed his water cup back down and finished off his fruit, and followed the man back down the corridor. He led Elji to the room where the others were still seated around the table, appearing silent yet content.

"Ahhh! Elji, you are awake." Dregar stood and came around to him. "Let me introduce you. These people are Bremen, Saloora, Elgred, and Charina."

Elji looked at them one by one and smiled. "It's good to meet you," he said. He was taken aback by the fact that Dregar had called one of the men Bremen. This was the "God on Earth." This was the man that every person he knew worshipped and talked about as the savior of them all. How his life had changed in such a short space of time, he thought.

"Come on, sit down," said the man Dregar had referred to as Bremen. "Let's eat and talk."

"It is no coincidence that we are all sitting here at this point," said Elgred. "We have conspired to bring together people that seem to have a direct impact on what is occurring, and who can influence the outcome of those things. What is interesting is that we have Elji with us. The rest of you were expected, and along with others were certainly part of the plan. The fact that Elji found the galrass and has been able to utilize it means, as we spoke about earlier, that something is affecting the flow of the universal essence that we were not aware of. And as we have already said, that in itself is a little worrying.

"Still, we are where we are, and we must make plans suited to what has happened so far. Some of us have been embroiled on this journey for a long time, but Saloora and Elji are new. It may well be a good idea for the sake of these two to lay out what is happening.

Elji, the Harood have told you some of the makeup of things, and I think that Saloora can learn these things as we go along to save having to repeat it.

"Here on this planet, we are in an eternal battle to try and focus the thoughts and minds of humans to ensure that they understand the makeup of the essence of the universe, and that they choose the path of good and right above and beyond that which is power and self-serving need. When we create a new civilization, our ultimate aim is to bring them to joining all other things in the universe. However, there are those that would try and derail this plan, and instill fledging societies with greed and avarice so that they can harness this and try and return and challenge the four.

"Framin and some of the worlds he has influenced have been on this path for longer than we need mention. He is here because this race is at a crossroads in the evolution of the species. If we are not careful, they will deviate from the path we need them to follow and the 'voice' of universal harmony and love will be gone, and we will have lost a race which I think has more promise than any we have nurtured in as long as I can remember. This society and people have the potential to become a real benefit to the universal essence. The fact that Framin is here means that he also sees the potential.

"We, The Four, decided pretty much in the beginning that when we were helping to create new life we would never directly involve ourselves in the consciousness of the people. Early in our journey of creation, when we did interfere, we created races that bypassed some of the learning they needed to join the essence. It seems there is no rushing the evolution of a species from an understanding perspective. Influencing their growth too much rushes this part of the evolution, and they never become whole to the universe. They need to evolve naturally, and at the pace that each species can manage."

He thought for a moment. "The universal lines of the essence that we use to watch all things are converging here. This has happened so rarely in the history of everything that we must take note. While all of this was our creation, it has been fed by all life as we know it, and so has a certain amount of unpredictability. We could, if needed, take hold of everything and orchestrate it all, but unless there is direct clarity that everything could fail, we will not do that. To create something is to give it its own life, and watch how that blossoms into something truly magnificent. We can't do this if we control all. Then it just becomes an extension of our capacity, and that, even though we have unimaginable capacity by your standards, would limit what might be possible.

"It would be very easy for us to believe that we can only allow what we want to allow and become like the gods many people worship. But we do not require recognition of control;

we just want to join in the enlightenment of all. Unpredictability is part of that.

"Could we have stopped the likes of Framin earlier on? Perhaps. But he adds to the growth of all things, as his desire creates those that oppose him and want to make things happen to ensure he doesn't succeed, and that in itself is a good thing. However, what we do know is that his overall ambition is to lift himself to the status of The Four, and that we cannot allow, as the unpredictability of it may be our undoing. So we work within the bounds we set to unseat him at every opportunity. He does have a hold here on this planet—he has been here for a long time, and has built something he spends a lot of energy hiding. That he has managed to do this is either because he has become more adept, or because something else is at play.

"What we do know is that we have an opportunity to undo his plans, and with luck blunt his ambition forever. This battle and his undoing is not one that can or should be waged by the collective essence alone. There must be something that is occurring here on this planet that has an influence, and we need to see it completed here. If we intervene we may lose something in the undoing that is of vital importance.

"The task is going to fall to you, and by you, I mean you, Bremen, and you, Saloora, and now Elji as well. Dregar and others will help where they can, and there will be others on the road that will no doubt lend weight to what you do, but because you are of the essence of this planet, it is you that must protect it.

"Charina and I will continue to spread hope and enlightenment through what we do, but we will not interfere unless it is absolutely necessary, and even then only in very dire need. You are the beings that will have to unravel and

87

bring to a conclusion what is happening here."

Charina looked at them. "Though we cannot and will not directly influence what happens here, we will lend whatever aid we can. There are two tasks that must be undertaken: one is that we must uncover what Framin is planning, and to do this you will travel to places you have never been. The second is that we must try and uncover if Ichancha is indeed at play somewhere here. It will be of importance in the overall scheme of the universal essence that we find her if she is indeed here somewhere.

"We know that you can't complete these things on your own, and as you travel you will find others who can help. The first thing we will do is show you the universal lines and how they all work and are connected, and as the need arises you can utilize this knowledge and travel to other worlds to learn and to recruit those to your undertaking."

Elji and Saloora had been listening to what had been said in silence, but Bremen had begun to fidget and become restless. "If I am to be involved in something that will take me away from Mehem, what will become of what we hope to accomplish here? How will we continue the work and the proliferation of the message if I am no longer here in person for the people to see?"

"We have thought of that," said Charina, and as she did she transformed in front of their eyes to be a duplicate of Bremen in every detail.

CHAPTER 13
BETHROD AND THE JALARIA

The huge fire pit burned hot and bright at the center of the lodge. Its sides were some five feet high, and were constructed of a tight metal mesh that held in all the wood and stone. Above the large brazier was a source of water that dripped onto the fire, generating huge clouds of steam and smoke. The smoke escaped through a small chimney placed above the brazier, while the steam, heavier in nature, rose and then fell. Still, there was the faint smell of wood smoke inside the lodge, tinged with the smell of herbs that were added as a ritual to ensure that this was not too overpowering.

Furs, horns, shields, and swords adorned the walls. Around the edges were pools filled with crystal clear hot water that sent steam into the air. Some of the pools bubbled and others were calm. Around the central fire was a pool, wheel shaped so that it surrounded it. This was filled with cold fresh water, and beyond the walls of the pool were wooden benches padded with materials and furs.

Men and women lounged in the pools and sat on the

benches nearest the fire. All were unclothed except for an occasional small slip, which covered the waist and nothing else.

Bethrod sat among this group of people; they were his warlords. Each of them controlled hundreds of warriors, both male and female, and each held sway over either a conquered land or a swathe of land within the realm. They were a rugged people, yet tall and fair haired. The men and the women fashioned long hair that was braided and hung loose. Most of the men sported beards that were also braided and decorated with small beads or bones. Their eyes were mainly blue and they had square-ish features, but even so they were a very handsome people.

Bethrod was the only one of a few amongst the race that was bronze skinned in color, but he was a fierce man and unbeaten in any battle. They had accepted him, as they believed he was touched by the gods, and he had never led them to a defeat. He was worshipped, feared, and adored at the same time.

These were his people, and he was immensely proud of their abilities and prowess as fighters, raiders, and conquerors. He was content to be amongst them. They were the Jalaria.

When he was young they were a fractured society of tribes who warred amongst each other either to gain land or resources from other tribes. He had coalesced them into a nation of cooperative warriors that now understood the benefit of working together. Even so, there were frequent battles between the tribes when it came to trying to prove who the greatest warrior tribe was, and many died or were taken during these skirmishes. They were much more infrequent now than in the past, and that was due in no part to his introduction of "priest warriors," or "Drendrak," as they were known. These were said to be the holders of the warlords' souls, kept in a chain of bones that they wore in a necklace called a graithe. They were seen as advisers and soothsayers. It was said that if they lost any of the bones from the graithe, the warlord in question lost some of his strength and influence. It was their task to ensure these were passed on from generation to generation, adding more bones to the graithe as time went on.

As each lord fathered a firstborn, each of these was also given a Drendrak, and they grew together and were keepers of the lore and the strength of each other, neither whole without the other.

Bethrod controlled each of the Drendrak though a universal cord, and was able to influence them to advise in the ways he required. All were ignorant of this fact except for Tragarg, who was the head of the Drendrak order, and brothered Bethrod himself.

It had been a slow undertaking, and Bethrod had been clever to introduce changes slowly and over many decades so that they became part of life. He was, by any standard, a clever, ambitious warrior.

Bethrod turned to his left and spoke to his closest commander, Harther. "Which of our brethren now plots my downfall? Is there still ambition amongst our warlords to disrupt the coalition? Or are they satisfied with their gains and the prospect of the chance to wage war and take another land?"

"There is always unrest, Bethrod," said Harther. "It is and has always been an uneasy alliance at best, held together by your ability to keep everyone engaged in some conquest or other. Still, having said that, there seems to be a settling in general of the lust for overall rule. It is now much more talk than action." He laughed. "Should you not be victorious in the open challenge tomorrow, I think we may face a different challenge."

"It is not my desire to let the work we have done so far crumble away to nothing. As much as I would like to defend my position, there are more important tasks to undertake. I will deal with that." He smiled a smile of someone completely sure of himself. "I hear through my sources that Lankan and his tribe were plotting to move higher up the chain of command, and he was about to challenge you."

"Yes, I had heard that," said Harther. "But I don't see much evidence of action. I think perhaps his bravado comes more from his consumption of ale than an actual desire to partake in such a risky venture." They both laughed.

As Bethrod turned to settle back, Gertia straddled his lap, ensuring she was pressed as far into him as she could be. "And what would my lord desire of his loyal subject today?" she asked, slowly working her hips from side to side. "Is there something I might be able to help him accomplish?" The smirk on her face was clear to see, and her hand was working towards the bottom of his stomach, circling as it went. She was by any stretch of the imagination a handsome woman, with strong, lithe features, breasts that were pert yet ample enough, and braided hair that cascaded long to her waist. The temptation was difficult to ignore, but he knew of her reputation for controlling those she bedded, and he was now used to her advances.

He quickly reversed their position so that he was on top of her, and he gave her a strong kiss and disentangled himself. She looked at him with a coy, lustful grin.

"Gertia," he said. "Your charms are not lost on me, but I am sure there are more deserving cases for your affections and needs here. Turn your attention to Harther here. I have heard he has more to give than most need."

"Yes," she said, looking sideways at Harther. "That I can vouch for." She laughed and sprung to her feet. "No fault. I will indeed find a more willing partner." And she moved away, leaving them all smiling.

"That woman may be the death of someone for sure," Harther commented.

Bethrod stood. "Brothers, sisters, the time has come for us to take more of what we desire. Our neighbors to the north and east have made an alliance with the god Framin, and he has promised them much. But he has also promised us much, and we will be first to strike and take that which we want. While we do his bidding and work for the cause, you all know we have a deeper plan to take all of that which he holds as his own and instill ourselves as the rightful and only rulers of the many realms. Once we have conquered our nearest allies, we will be able to move further afield till we own and rule all that we can imagine. It is our birthright, and only we, the true Jalaria, are smiled upon by the true gods. It is time to throw off our shackles of perceived servitude to this false god and take what we want."

The room erupted in noise and cheers and the raucous rattling of wall shields and spears.

"Tomorrow we gather the armies of the Jalaria and we go to conquest and victory. No one can stand before us, and all those that do will be trodden down beneath the feet of the true lords of the free world."

Again the room erupted.

"Now go and provision your warriors; we have far to go and much to take."

At that Bethrod walked towards the rear of the room and through the door, followed by Tragarg.

"That was a risky announcement," Tragarg said. "What if Framin feels the disruption in the lines?"

"I suspect that Framin will feel the vibrations of a nation willing to murder and pillage that will fuel his need. My trace on him revealed something to me that we need to speak of, and I need you to gather the Drendrak. We must use them to influence their lords. We have a need to swap sides, and quickly. See it done, and bring them to the great hall."

Tragarg left to do his bidding and Bethrod made his way to the hall. There was time to see Kreanna, he thought, before he talked with the Drendrak.

***

Tragarg went out the door and down the street towards the Drendrak lodge. It was a building hexagonal in shape, and constructed of thick stiff oak beams and a glistening kind of stone that gave off its own light. Other than that, it looked small and inconsequential

He approached the door, which was framed and barred by bones and skeletons of long dead brothers of the tribes. His graithe glowed as he got close, and an opening appeared between the bones. He entered, turned left, and headed down into rooms carved into the earth. The rooms ran on and on and twisted and turned. If you did not know the route it would be easy to become confused and end up where you had started.

His brothers all lived here when they were gathered — indeed, this was their base, and possessions of importance were left here at all times when not needed. Each of them also left a small part of their graithe, which was woven into a large wreath held in the central repository. This enabled each of them to be able to return here if they were in any kind of trouble that they could not contain. It held a part of their universal essence.

He entered the central room, took hold of the wreath, and called his brothers. They appeared one by one till they were all in attendance.

"It is time," he said. "Time to take that which is rightfully ours; time to hide our true nature and influence our lords for the greater good."

They all joined each other by removing their graithes, each one grasping that of the brother next to him till they formed a complete circle.

Tragarg imparted the plan to them all at the same time, sharing the detail and the vision. When he had finished they all left by the same means they had arrived, and he was once again left alone. He turned and began to make his way back to Bethrod. This was indeed a time of danger and chance.

***

Kreanna was sitting in their chamber, her son, their eldest, close by in a chair. She jumped up and embraced Bethrod long and hard after he entered. "Thank you," she whispered. "Thank you for knowing and sparing our son."

Bethrod smiled at his son. "There are things that Framin thinks he controls that are always discoverable if you know where to look. He is foolish in his belief that he understands all; it is his weakness in all of this. We are lucky enough to have discovered that it is in our compassion for all things that we can utilize the true essence, He is blinded by his hatred of The Four. He does not and can never discover what we know and our connection to them through Dregar.

"That is enough of such talk. Let's sit and talk of a world where we can be free to follow those things we most want, a world of love and hope in all things. If all goes to plan, soon we will be free of the tyranny of death and hatred. Then we will grow and prosper and be truly free."

"You risk much in doing this thing," said Kreanna. "Must our son go?"

"The others are already gathering in Mehem. They will need his strength and his knowledge, His skills as a warrior are only surpassed by me—I have taught him everything I know.

"It's time, Cloin—it's time to take up your task. Where is your sister Naimer?" As he spoke her name she appeared. "Make your way to Mehem, both of you. Join the others and find out what your task might be. You must give them all your strength and power. Your mother and I are proud of you, and your heritage is strong. We have taught you both what it is to be one with the essence, but you will learn more. Go in peace and love."

Cloin and Naimer looked at their parents, joined hands, and faded from sight.

Kreanna said, "I hope we know what we are doing—I hope we are right in what we do."

"My love," Bethrod said. "We can never know; we can only do what we must."

They stood together staring at the empty space for what seemed an age.

Tragarg came in and stood by them both. "It is done," he said. "The Drendrak have begun the task of disrupting the plans of Framin. Many of our people will not return from this. We sacrifice everything for the good of a future we are unlikely to see. Still, better to fall in battle than to stand by and do nothing."

Again they fell silent....

ELJI AND THE GALRASS

CHAPTER 14
OF WORLDS AND ALLIANCES.

Elgred, Charina, Dregar, Bremen, Elji, and Saloora stood in the very center of the quadrangle, and above them was what appeared to be a larger version of Elji's galrass, though it wasn't constrained by an outer shell.

"Are we going to be on the move again?" asked Elji.

"Yes," said Elgred. "It is time to make alliances with those that will help. The Jalaria have started their journey to disrupt Framin's plans, and you must help them where you can. Bethrod has sent his son and daughter, Cloin and Naimer, to join us, and we must all now go about our separate tasks in the hope that as a whole we can shift the balance of what is to come.

"Dregar, you will go with Elji back to your home world of Quandium, and see what they know there and what help we may get. Then, if you can, you should go and visit the Harood again, but this time on their world. They may know something that they do not think to tell us. Once you are done in those places, come back and meet the others at the confluence of the river Arl, at the foot of the hills from where Framin plots and schemes. Be wary, all of you; he will not be easy to fool, and his power and hold on the essence is very strong.

"Saloora and Bremen, your task is to visit the cities of each of the eleven remaining Gouarong and try and untangle the universal lines. If you can somehow turn them to tune in more to hope than hate, it will have a great impact on the fate of the others.

"Charina and I will wait for Cloin and Naimer. I had thought to send them with you two, but I think they must go down a different path and seek out what we know of Ichancha. It may be that they have little part to play in what is to come in the near future, but I think it worth the risk."

"Let me show you how this works," Dregar said to Elji, and he took his hand and moved it towards the lines. They put their finger on a line and Dregar dragged his finger along it to a point. They vanished.

Bremen and Saloora looked at Elgred, and he nodded. "You two will be in grave danger, but you must follow the lines and see where they converge. Your strength in the bond you have will perhaps enable you to change the tune of the essence lines in these places, and so undo some of the hatred that has been instilled in the people of those lands where the convergences lie. You must uncover where they are hidden and do your best."

Bremen took Saloora's hand, closed his eyes, and began a low singing chant. She felt the hairs on the back of her neck start to stand and they disappeared.

Charina and Elgred were left alone and turned to leave the quadrangle. As they did they felt the arrival of Cloin and Naimer. They found them standing in one of the rooms off the main hallway

"Welcome!" said Elgred. "Welcome indeed. It is good to

see you both here. How is your father?"

It was Cloin that answered. "He is well. Even though he is worried he does not show it. It seems there is a lot at stake, and he and Mother still think of us both as children. As such they would rather keep us safe than see us involved this deeply. We are more capable than they know, but that doesn't stop them feeling as they do." Cloin smiled. "Not knowing what we are about to embark on does not help. Have you decided yet how we can help?"

"Yes," said Charina. "Elgred and I have thought about this, and we believe there is someone we must find that can help us to tip the balance in our favor. Let's sit down and we can tell you what we need of you."

They all moved towards the back of the room and sat on low, soft, covered cushions.

"Has your father told you anything of who we are?" Elgred asked.

"Yes," said Naimer. "He has told us what he knows, and we have gleaned more from watching the essence lines. We understand the challenge we face, and the danger of what may unfold for our world."

"I suspect," said Elgred, "that there is still much you don't know, but perhaps it is not needed that you understand the detail. When we were first starting to create things in the universe, there were more of us than just Charina and myself. However, things transpired over the millennia where we lost connection from the universal essence of someone we think may have a part to play in all this. We have not felt her presence for a long time, but there seems to be something that we may yet find that could lead us to her. Charina and I have felt the tiniest flicker of something we think means that Ichancha may be here on this planet, but not in the same form as we knew her. We need you to find her, and see what you can learn about what she does and what she knows.

"Once, many eons ago when there were the four of us, something happened to Lhapso that meant his energy was absorbed into the whole of the universe. At this time we did not really understand how this had happened, as we were and are the creators of all things. But his essence, when it dissipated into the all, brought about eons of peace and quiet, and allowed us to create civilizations that were peaceful and helpful to us in the creation of all things. Ichancha also lost herself to the universe as a whole, but with her it was somewhat different, and we are sure that somewhere she exists but in a form we don't recognize. While she has some influence it is important that we find her, as her control may have more of an impact than we, and indeed she, knows. The only thing we can tell is that she is somewhere far to the northeast of us. The essence of her we feel is so faint it's almost nonexistent, and is very different from the essence of the true Ichancha. We can let you see what we know, and transfer the signature to you to help find it. We are hoping that with Naimer's knowledge and use of the graithe and its collective strength, you may be able to discover her.

"She will not know who she is, and you may find it a very difficult task to persuade her of her true identity. Though I think you have the skill. Because we don't know the situation she is in, we felt it better to have you go with Naimer, Cloin, in case there is some danger surrounding her. Even if we can glean a little of what she may know, it might help us to understand more about what is happening."

Cloin looked at Elgred and Charina. "My skills are those of

a warrior, and Naimer is more than able to take care of herself in most situations. Do you not think that the cause may be better served if I go to where we know there may be trouble?"

"We don't know what situation Ichancha may be in," said Charina, "and two people undertaking a task means it is far more likely to succeed than if one goes alone. If it turns out that there is no need for your particular skills where you go, I am sure that you will be able to join the others where you are most needed when the time comes. But for now, I think it important you help to protect your sister and find out what you can."

"In all that's going on," said Cloin, "it just seems that we are being given something to do that doesn't suit our skills."

Elgred stood up from the cushion and waved his hands in the air. It became black, a void that was so totally devoid of anything that could be considered in the human perception of things that it was mind numbing. A voice came into their heads.

"There was a world here once much like Earth; now it is nothing—it is absent of anything that could be considered even space. This world was watched by Ichancha. She nurtured and created all the life forms on it. They were beautiful and regal and peace loving. They were not beings as you know them, but they were sentient all the same. They were made from the very fabric of the universe. They were powerful, compassionate, and generous of nature. But something happened here, something even we can't fathom, and in its happening we lost Ichancha. All we can describe it as for you is that she dissipated. She was absorbed by something none of us knew was even created. It was not created by any of us. So we must assume that somehow, something she did or tried to do caused this to happen.

"I am going to remove a barrier now, as I want you to feel the only thing that seems to be here. It will be for a mere fraction of time, but it will be enough."

The desolation crushed them. All at once they felt that every fiber of their being was infected with a blackness that could not even be named or felt, yet it was there. Their bones began to crumble, their skin to peel away. They shrieked in anguish and pain, overwhelmed by feelings of doom and destruction.

Suddenly they were back.

"That was not even a timeframe that can be measured small enough by your comprehension, but I am sure you felt an eternity of something. We don't know what this nothing is, or how it even became to be registered on a scale we can comprehend. We can't be sure that this wasn't created by Ichancha somehow. Or if it came and took her away from what we consider to be all creation. What we do know is that this world's void now lies in a black hole, a dead star. We, The Four, have never created these things, yet they are here and therefore we must heed their existence.

"Since we lost Ichancha we have tried to understand these things, but we lack something that we think she may know. Only she may be able to tell us what happened.

"What we can't allow is for Framin or his followers to become aware of the existence of this. We really fear that they would try and utilize it somehow to drive everything in existence to what we can only consider as nothing. At the very least this could tip the balance of probability of the existence of the human race towards destruction, hatred, and death. We have no idea how it may be used. We have no idea if it even can be used, but we cannot even let it be a possibility that such a thing may happen.

"Now do you see why we need her? Now do you see the importance of finding out if she still is or has any kind of essence left? We don't know where you may have to go to find her or what you may face. You don't go to just find her—you go to unravel something deeper and more complicated than anything we have knowledge of so far in the creation of all things. We can't assume, then, that there is nothing either defending or influencing what the outcome of her return might be. It's not without thought that we send you two on this particular task."

Cloin and Naimer both nodded. "OK, we understand," Naimer said. "We will do this thing, and either bring her back or discover what else may be involved, and therefore ease the battle to come."

"Good," said Elgred. "Now, let us give you what we know of her signature in the essence." He placed a hand on each of their shoulders, and in an instant, they knew what they looked for.

"Thank you," said Cloin. "Is there anything else we should know before we go?"

"No," said Elgred. "Now it's in your hands. You know where we are if needed. Reach out whenever you think we may be able to help. Otherwise we will wait for your call."

They both stood, joined hands again, and faded from sight.

Charina looked at Elgred. "It used to be easier when we could just influence all this ourselves," she said to him.

"Yes, it was, but then we would never have been able to create such diversity and have all these beings aid us in what we do. They may just discover something we can't. That is why we decided on the principle of adding chaos into the creation of life in the first place. It has both negative and positive effects, and everything is so much more interesting." He smiled at her and they sat again.

"It will be interesting to see if what we do now allows us

to move forward to the timeline we know can be, or if it will be different," Charina said.

"Interesting yes, but at this moment impossible to tell. Having to move in a way that is measured adds a dimension that causes some interesting problems." He laughed.

"What concerns me most is the fact that we have to be circumspect with what we tell everyone. Getting people to do your bidding by not telling the truth is a little alien." He tilted his head. "Still, we do what we must."

CHAPTER 15
INTO THE UNKNOWN

Bremen and Saloora arrived outside the City of Spires. Bremen knew this was where Kahilja resided, and he thought it best to start at the very heart of something rather than try and learn what they might from far away.

Somewhere hidden in the city there had to be a place where the essence lines were controlled by Kahilja, and that was what they needed to find. They needed to be careful though — these people were fierce and bloodthirsty. He knew that Saloora didn't have much experience with people other than those she had met so far in her own land and in Mehem, and they had not had time for her to gain an understanding of all other lands and their people from the information they had stored in his palace. She would just have to trust him that this was the place to start, and follow his lead on how to deal with these people.

The air was cold. Snow lay around in small pockets and was stirred by a wind that seemed to bite through to the bone. Bremen clothed them in furs and stout leather britches, provided them both with fur lined boots to match, and covered their heads with flat leather fur lined caps. Their natural hair would arouse suspicion here, so he changed their appearance to be darker and more swarthy in nature. In short, he disguised them as members of the general populace of this cold land to try and blend in as much as possible.

"We should find somewhere to stay, and then see what we can learn about what is happening in the city. After that, we need to find the best way of getting into the central part of the city and as close to the lines as possible without arousing suspicion, none of which is going to be easy," Bremen said.

"I agree. Somewhere warm would be nice," Saloora said, and she laughed.

"We should pose as mercenaries looking for work, and be as unspecific as possible about where we are from. We both have the ability to speak their language—Elgred has given us the ability to understand and speak any we need without thought, so there will be no danger of being misunderstood. It is unusual but not unheard of for women to become warriors here. It is a harsh land and the women are tough and strong, but mainly their duties are to breed and keep the camps going. A female, whether a warrior or not, will be seen as fair game unless she is tithed to a warrior herself. So for the sake of our journey you will have to be my tithed warrior maid." He smiled at her. "Not something I suspect suits your nature, but for my part, if it's another chance to be close to you I will take it—it does have a certain appeal." He smiled.

Saloora laughed. "Bremen, there is much you don't know about me. While I have not had much experience with men, I have lived with a lion pride, and I know the hierarchy and the behavior. I think it will suit this situation well. Now, if you're telling me I have to obey your every command, then we may have a problem."

He laughed then too. "Don't worry. I will be gentle with you." They both laughed together at that. "Come on, let's go to the city and find some lodgings."

They walked through a gate and into the city, which was dirty and cold. The ground was halfway between wet and frozen, and mud was everywhere. Huddled in corners and doorways were people looking miserable, ill fed, and clothed in rags hardly useful in repelling the cold. The cold wind had a low whistle that added to the misery of the place. As they walked they heard a noise, and just had time to flatten themselves against the side of a poorly constructed building before a troop of well armored riders stormed past, taking little care as to who was in their way. It was clear that there was little if any order in this part of the city, and the tension was palpable.

Pulling themselves away from the wall they continued their walk, and soon heard voices raised to a level that was near shouting. They could see a gathering of people standing outside a building that might pass for an inn. A sign swinging in the wind was held to the wall above the door by one metal hinge, and had the faded image of a black donkey coming down a ramp from what appeared to be a ship. Letters underneath the picture were so faded they could not be seen.

They headed toward it, and as they tried to enter they were blocked by a number of surly looking men, all clothed in what could only be considered sailors' dress. Some were even barefooted in the cold. It was clear that they had either been there for some time and had drank their fill already, even though it was early morning, or that they had made their way here from some other establishment ready to continue their drinking.

"What have we here?" said one of the men. Short but wide shouldered, he had a beard that was prodigious in its length and thickness. "Two pretty birds bringing us some coin to continue our drinking." He stepped even closer to Saloora. She grabbed him by the arm, and before anyone could do anything she had him pinned against the wall and was holding a dagger across his throat.

"I assume you lead these men?" she hissed into his ear. "I suggest that you tell them we want no trouble here, if you value your throat." At that she spun him around, causing a small tear in the skin of his throat, and had her knife levelled back at his throat again.

"Oh! We have a feisty one here," he said, and as he did he tried to push his head back to release himself from Saloora. She was too quick, and with a couple of flicks and twists she had him face down on the ground, her knee in his back and a foot pinning his hand to the floor. This time her dagger was over one of his fingers, and she pressed and cut it off just above the knuckle. He screamed.

"Perhaps I didn't make myself clear," she said, and positioned her knife over one of his other fingers. "Now, should we start again?"

"He does not lead us" said one of the men that had been standing in the group as he came forward. He was a lean, thin faced man, slight and wiry, but held a sparkle in his eye that hinted he was very dangerous. "Now, we don't want any trouble here—Weerlam was just toying with you. If you could give him back his finger, we could go inside get a drink and talk about this misunderstanding." He smiled. "I am Florin, and for my sins I lead this band of mother lovers. Come on now, let's talk." With that he turned and entered the inn.

Saloora let the man go and stood. She and Bremen walked in after Florin. He had moved to a table tucked away in the back corner of the room. The room itself smelled of cheap gin and beer. The floors were sticky with the spills, and sawdust had been thrown around to soak up as much as possible. Seated all around were men who looked like they would sooner slit your throat as talk to you.

"You chose a difficult place to try and make friends and take a rest," said Florin. "I take it you're not from this city or anywhere nearby? If I can give you a bit of advice, it's that you should be very careful as to where you walk about. Still, I can see you have some skill, and don't seem to be phased by confrontation. Now, let's talk about what you are doing here, and why I shouldn't indicate to the rest of my men in this establishment and have you chopped into pieces." He then showed an evil grin that left them in no doubt that he was not just trying to scare them with his bravado. He had the air of a man very confident in his ability to carry out what he promised.

Bremen and Saloora looked around again, and could see that most eyes were on them. They were outnumbered at least 30 to 1.

Bremen said, "Florin, we don't mean any disrespect to anyone, and we were only trying to secure some lodgings. We had heard that there was need of mercenaries in this city, and our plan was to get settled and then try to ply our trade. My friend Saloora here has a habit of acting on instinct, and at the best of times she doesn't take well to being threatened.

"If it helps, she could have killed him and the rest of your men outside without too much trouble, and the fact that she didn't means she is in a good mood." He smiled then. "Make no mistake, though you think the odds are stacked in your favor, I truly believe we have more than a 50/50 chance of leaving this place with you all lying on the floor." He also smiled then, and his grin was equally as convincing in its surety as that of Florin.

Florin let out a high-pitched laugh at that. It broke the ice in the room and the noise increased, and people went back to their drinking and talking.

"My new friends," he said. "Let me tell you the situation you have walked into and what is happening in this city."

He waved his hand at a barmaid, and she came over bringing three flagons of ale. "I know from the outside this establishment may be a bit tawdry, but the ale is great, and it does take a lot of work to get a place to look this bad. It wouldn't do for us to have everyone just wandering in off the street—it serves a purpose to have it seem like a den of ill repute. But the food is actually as good as the ale, and the rooms around back are as good as any you will get in the city, and for half the price.

"So...for you to be as sure as you seem to be about your abilities, you are either fools, can wield some kind of magic, or you are as good as you say you are. At this point I don't need to know which, but seeing as you are here I would like to know what it is you are trying to do here, and see if there is some profit in it for us." At that he lifted his flagon of ale and drank

Saloora and Bremen glanced at each other and did the same. Bremen was weighing up what he ought to tell this man they had just met, so he studied him and soaked up the essence of the man's core to see where his true self lay. What he felt surprised him. This man was indeed a leader, and what's more he had been moving children out of this and other cities for many months and taking them to places of safety using ships that he and his men owned. Bremen decided then that he could be trusted, to a point, with at least some of the truth, and perhaps he could find out the full extent of what they were up to and how they might help each other. Strange, he thought, how fate could bring you into contact with the most unlikely of people. He laughed inside. He was sure that Elgred must have known something of this, and it was why they had started in this place. He put down his flagon of ale and leaned forward

"In truth," said Bremen, "We have been watching what is going on here and in other cities, and we've come to find out as much information as we can and see how we can help, as there seems to be a lot of needless suffering going on. We need, somehow, to get into the central part of the city, and probably the palace, find out where Kahilja is, and see what we can discover. What do you know or what can you tell us?"

Florin sat back and thought for a moment. "This is a time of much mistrust, and while I have no reason to doubt what you say, we have had many people come to us and say they need help. Now, I am not saying I may or may not be able to help you, but the price will have to be right, and I need to know I can trust you not to try and dupe us out of some coin. If you really need my help, I think the best way to go forward is for me to get you some rooms here. Then I would like you to meet me down at the main docks on the lake at midnight. Look for a building with a sign of a hook and anchor on it, and wait there—I will find you. Now come on, let's get you that room."

Florin stood, beckoned for the waitress again, and the three of them left the room.

Florin was as good as his word, and had taken them to a room around the back that was both comfortable and clean. It had an exit in the back of the building, where he told them they would be able to come and go with much more privacy than using the main entrance to the building. He had left them there, and reminded them where and when to meet him.

"Do you think we can trust him?" asked Saloora when he had gone.

"Well," said Bremen. "We had little choice in our actions, based on the situation you put us in with that little stunt, and seeing as we are in the predicament we are in, I suppose it's logical to see it through to the end. In any case, how much more trouble could we possible get in that we can't resolve? I, for one, am going to try and get some rest. I am cold and I am tired. I suggest you do the same."

"You're right—let's do that," said Saloora, and they made themselves comfortable to wait. In no time they were asleep, both feeling confident they would wake in time to go and meet Florin.

It was dark as they both left the back of the building. Florin had given them directions from the inn, and they made their way down the back streets, keeping to the shadows while being as cautious as possible, all the time heading for the big lake where the docks were situated. It was even more bitterly cold than it had been through the day, but they were rested and still wrapped up warmly.

There was a silent hush around the city, a feel that most sensible people were tucked up inside and didn't wish to venture out in this part of town at this time of night. They could see the spires that projected from the main central building, and all the other spires that came from buildings around the central one. The proliferation of these spires was where the city had got its name, and in times gone by they were used for hailing the populace and calling them to prayer. For years now they had been silent, and in that silence had taken on a foreboding feel, seeming to glow black like obsidian in the pale moonlight.

They turned a corner and headed down the last alley towards the building that Florin had described. They could see the sign as he had described, and just beneath it bales and an opening that would allow them to wait out of sight.

All round the entrance, and at the buildings on either side up and down the street, they could see small, crane like contraptions that had hooks on the ends of sturdy ropes. It was clear that these were used to load produce and baskets and bales from boats to wagons that edged the road that ran directly up to the city from the lake.

They approached and began to hunker down out of sight. As they did, from above dropped a large net. As they started to shout and stand it fell on them, and through some property or other rendered them senseless.

Saloora and Bremen came to their senses, and they could feel that their heads had been covered in some kind of cloth and their hands were tied behind them with some kind of rope that, as they squirmed, got tighter and tighter.

"I wouldn't squirm if I were you," came a voice. "Those ropes were given to us by the Klormrand that live in the woods way to the east of the city across the lake. They have properties that seem to stop anyone from using anything that might be considered not normal. They will tighten the more you move."

Bremen sighed; he had had enough. He stood and lost all his bonds, as well as his hood, in one swift movement. As he did so he looked around and sent out waves of calm and quiet. He could see two people in the room. One was Florin, and the other an older man who was small and well dressed. They both looked at him in surprise, but stayed where they were.

"Now we have met," said Bremen. "Let's see what we can discover." He touched Saloora and all her ropes and hood

113

disappeared. With lightning speed she was behind the men, and had both held by one arm that was painful to even look at.

"It's OK, Saloora—I think we will get cooperation." She let go and both men rubbed their arms and sat.

"You weren't joking at the inn when you said the odds were not in my favor, were you?" said Florin.

"No," said Bremen. "Though we would prefer to make friends rather than enemies. In times such as these we all need friends." He thought for a moment. "I know of your work to try and free the children of the city, and I really would like to understand what is happening here and see if we can help. We are not here to undo any of your plans, and indeed, it would benefit you greatly to have us on your side. There are things and people we know that can help you in what you try and achieve if we can just understand it."

The two men looked at each other, and the older one shrugged his shoulders.

"I am Jalad," said the old man. "Florin here is my son. We have been transporting goods around the great lake that serves this city for many years. In recent times we have seen a great darkness start to take hold in this city, and in the others that stand on the shores of the lake.

"There was a time I can remember as a boy when the City of Spires was a great place, a wonder to behold. It sparkled, and was full of life. Sure, there was poverty and danger, but it was controlled and more a rarity than a common occurrence. Over time, though, the city and its people have lost their reason to live. Food is scarce, money is tight, belief has gone, and those that try and stand up have their children taken away from them. The children are taken into the city palace and never seen again. Many say that Kahilja uses them to perform dark magic that seems to fall over the city and suck the life from its people. We have always had contracts with the palace to transport goods and men around the lake, and we have used this influence to move children away from the city and to the forest lands, where the Klormrand live. They are a kind, good people that seem to have the ability to hide from the despair and are very rarely seen. If you can truly help us start to put an end to this hopelessness, we will help you." He looked at them both with hope

"We do have access, as I said, to the palace, and we can get you into it without much trouble. We can't give you much, if any, help once you are in. One of our people once reported that he was taken to a room that pulsated with light right in the very heart of the palace. He said that they made him remove bodies of dead women and children by the dozen. He only went the once, and after he reported it to us we never saw him again.

"We have built ourselves a reputation as a group that is firmly in tune with the powers that rule, and they believe us to be co-conspirators. That way they tend to leave us alone. That is what you saw when you came across the inn. It's a façade that works pretty well.

"I am sorry you were treated so poorly, but we couldn't risk exposing what it is we do, and it is the only way we can be sure. If we had discovered you were not who you say you were, you would never have left this room alive. So…," he said, looking at them both again. "How can you help us? And who are you?"

Bremen dropped their disguises, and it was Saloora who spoke. "This is Bremen, and I am Saloora. We are part of a group of people who want to see the world put back in order, and for peace and prosperity to begin to take hold again. We

115

know that your lord Khilja serves a being named Framin. He is one of twelve across the world that serve him. Their aim is to cover the world in darkness and despair, and we must stop him. To do this we need to get to this room you speak of. Once there, we need time to be able to discover what it is and how it is connected to others. If you can get us in, we can do the rest. It would be good, though, to have a distraction while we try and do this. How many men do you have?"

"We have more than two-hundred men here in this city, and probably another fifty scattered around the other cities of the lake," Florin said.

"And how many men control the city?" asked Bremen.

"Not many more than three-thousand. I wouldn't think, and of those around five-hundred personal guards that patrol the palace."

Bremen thought, "Do you think it might be possible to use your men to create some havoc down around the docks here, sufficient enough that the palace would have to respond to quell anything?"

"Possible, yes," said Florin. "But the response would be swift, and we would lose many men." He thought for a moment. "Perhaps if we could get to the palace fleet and set it alight, it may cause a ruckus and many of them to come running to save the fleet…. Yes, that may be a plan, and it wouldn't need many of our men and would put only a few in danger."

"I would suggest," said Bremen, "that you could also do the same in areas of the city that are uninhabited. We don't want to cause any risk to the people, but that may be unavoidable. The chaos would allow us extra distraction to get into the main palace.

"How long do you think it would take to get the word out

to your men?"

"We have a network and a system of getting messages along swiftly," said Jalad. "I think we could have a plan in place by sunset tomorrow."

"Good," said Saloora. "You know, I think we have the beginnings of a plan."

Jalad, Florin, and Bremen all looked at her.

"I think you're enjoying this," said Bremen.

"No, I wouldn't call it enjoyment," said Saloora. "But I can sense that this plan might work, and that is something to be cheerful about."

"OK," said Florin. "Now what can you do for us?"

"Well," said Bremen. "If we can make sure that we unsettle what is happening here, that will certainly ease life in general for everyone, just as a start. I could set up the ability to be able to move people quickly from the city to where you transport the children. If that is to the Klormrand at the eastern end of the lake? We will have to be careful though—if people start disappearing from the city en masse, it could arouse suspicion, and may undo what we are both trying to do."

"Yes," said Florin "we take the children and what women we can to the Klormrand. Where they live doesn't seem to be affected at all by what is going on in the cities around the lake, and as a people they are more than happy to have their lands inhabited by children. They are an amazing people, and we certainly wouldn't want to put any of them at risk. You are right, we need to be careful how we do this, but any help would be really appreciated. I think it depends on how much destruction you think is coming to the city."

"Let's see what we can discover in the palace, and base a plan around what we think the outcome of any confrontation might be. Then we can decide on what best suits everyone," said Bremen. "If it all goes to plan there will be no need to move people at all. When do you think might be the best time to try and get into the palace?"

"If we can get the word out now, I think with a bit of luck and some planning we could get you into the palace tomorrow after dark, and then start to cause some chaos. It will also give us time to consider how we might be able to help as many as possible," Jalad said.

"Perfect," said Bremen. "In which case we have some time, so Saloora and I are going to tell you as much as we know, and help enlighten you about what we do and its importance."

Bremen and Saloora began to tell the tale of The Four, and how all life is created and nurtured. Jalad and Florin sat in complete silence. It seemed they could not believe what they had just heard as told by Bremen and Saloora. They were astounded, amazed, and yet seemed to grasp a basic truth in what was said, and could see the need.

"So," said Saloora. "Now you know the sum of it. Clearly there is much more to tell, but the basics are there for you to grasp. Now that you know, how do you feel?"

Bremen could see that their faces were covered with confusion, but, as many times before when he had told the truth of all things, he could see relief, wonder, and hope written on their faces as well.

"It's astounding," said Florin. "Truly astounding. Can we really be in such a situation as this, to have everything we need within our grasp if we can but see it and believe it? It's almost too much to believe in itself. There is one thing for certain, however, and that is that even if I were to believe in only a small portion of what you say, then I would pledge all the resources we have to help. How could we not if the possible outcome is for all humanity to be aligned as one? Amazing...." He began to splutter.

Bremen laughed. "The story has that effect on a lot of people, and it will take time and probably thousands of questions for you to be able to fully embrace the enormity yet simplicity of what we have told you. We can talk when all this is over, but in the meantime, if it's OK with you, Saloora and I will return to our room and get some rest before we begin."

"Yes, yes of course," said Florin. "We will come to the inn later and let you know how we have progressed."

Bremen and Saloora made their way back to the inn and entered through the back door into their room. They were tired but exhilarated at the same time, feeling like they had made progress on what was to be done, and had in the process found some allies.

They had re-established their disguises as they walked back in case they were seen, but now back in the room Bremen dropped them again. Saloora sighed and turned back to look at Bremen. "I think and hope that we have achieved something today that will help, I feel like it has."

Bremen stepped closer to her, then ran his arm round her waist and pulled her in close. "We have done and will always do what we can," he said, then kissed her.

She tingled at his touch and the touch of his lips on hers and responded in kind. At that moment their souls intertwined, and for the first time they lost themselves in each other.

CHAPTER 16
QUANDIUM

Dregar and Elji appeared on the world of Quandium on the edge of a wide-open space, which was shimmering and emitting a note that was so basic it was as if it was resonating against Elji's bones. It had a deep comforting resonance that filled Elji with hope and joy.

Dregar moved forward and Elji followed him. As they walked the ground flexed and dipped with the pressure of their weight. Dregar stopped, closed his eyes, and sat down. Elji looked at him, shrugged his shoulders, now used to Dregar's strange actions, and thought he ought to do the same.

"This," said Dregar, "is the essence of the whole of the race to which I belong. They do not exist now as corporeal beings, but are part of the resonance of the whole universe. There are actually less than what might be considered one hundred entities left now, as most through the passing of time have joined with other times and planes. Those that are no longer here, though, have left their collective knowledge. We are able to resolve ourselves into beings as you see me now, but I think in this instance it will just be easier for us to join with them. We will leave our bodies here—they will be perfectly safe. We will create a reality that is familiar to your frame of reference, and the rest of my kin will appear in your mind in some human form like me. We will try and create something that is meaningful so that you can see how we interact with everything in the universe."

The space materialized around Elji, and it was familiar yet still held an ethereal quality. They were in a room much like the interior of a temple of some kind. Not that Elji had been in a temple before, but he had heard tales of such. Around the edges were impressive pillars that reached right up to a very clear blue sky. The floor still seemed to be pulsating, but was much more solid, as if made of marble. Chairs and a very large round table were situated in the center of the room, and in each chair were beings that were human like in their appearance but regal looking. They were slender and tall, clothed in shifts that covered all but their arms and head. Each of them had what appeared to be blue hair, but on closer inspection was more like a collection of small electrical blue charges, much like Elji had seen in the galrass.

"Welcome, Dregar," said the being that was seated nearest to them. "We haven't seen you for many a century, and it's good to have you here. We have missed your constant presence and disruptive force." He smiled, and Dregar moved towards him and they embraced. "And who is this you have with you?"

"Elji," said Dregar, "this is Amaran. You might consider him to be my brother, though such family alliances died out among our race many centuries ago. Thank you, Amaran. It is indeed good to be back."

Elji continued to look around, and noticed that the beings

at the table were both male and female in form. Those furthest from him were more transparent than those closest, but he noticed that when he shifted his gaze he could see that they all glowed the faintest of glows. The rest of the room itself had little reference to anything he knew, except for the fact that it had walls, though as noticed earlier the ceiling was open to the skies.

"You know," said Dregar, "of where I have been for the last few centuries, and how I have been helping Elgred and Charina with the direction and hope for the human race. Well, things are happening that seem bent on derailing all the work we have put in. Framin has a hand in this, and is trying to influence the awakening of the race and move it towards the thing he has tried to do on other worlds, where hate and despair are the prevalent forces. Elji here has become entangled in the process. He has found a galrass, and as such has earned himself a place amongst the destiny of human kind. He seems to have the knack and an understanding at the core of his being about what we do and what everything is, and how to manipulate the essence of the universe. How this is we are not sure, but it is what it is and here he is. I am hoping we might discover who had a hand in Elji finding the galrass and what it means. We also need to gather as much information as we can about the powers that are trying to influence the universal lines of the earth. That is why we are here.

"We could do with your help to uncover what we can about Framin's plans, see who, if anyone, assists him, and see what we may need to do to regain the upper hand on influencing the course of the human race."

Amaran and the others around the table nodded to one another, and he spoke.

"You know, Dregar, that we cannot influence anything that happens in the universe—we do not have the knack for it. We do as we have always done since we ascended to be in tune with the universal essence, and that is that we watch. There has only ever been you of our kind that has made the decision to directly involve themselves in the affairs of a race's ascendance. Still, we will do what we can. Come and sit down, and let's begin."

Elji and Dregar sat and around the table the beings began to join hands. As they did notes of different levels and pitch began to sound and harmonize with each other, creating a song, a concerto of sound, a thing of utter beauty and promise so fundamental Elji felt himself slipping into something, and visions appeared.

"This is where everything exists and where everything is joined. Here is where all things either in existence or things that might be in existence are. This is where all possibilities lie. Everything is here, joined by the fact that all things come from the one thing."

He could see a myriad of lines and specs, each connecting to each other. As he looked at each spec he could see a world, and as he looked closer at a world he could see a hundred more exact worlds stretching off into the distance, connected to each other.

"What you are seeing," said Amaran, "are the infinite future timelines of each of the worlds. The longer you look at them the more of them you will see. Remember, all things are possible; therefore these are infinite. If you do not have the power to control how you look, you could be swept into this infinite loop and never return. It seems, though, as Dregar has said, you have some basic understanding inbuilt. The lines you see are just a representation by your mind of the connection of the universal essence to all things. In reality it is everywhere, but it suits everyone's purpose to imagine each as a line. That way we can follow it—otherwise we also would be lost in the chaos of possibility. Now let's find the earth."

The image in front of them swirled and twisted. Visions swept past, and he caught glimpses of things he couldn't even comprehend, let alone explain. Things came back into focus and he was looking at what he considered must be the earth. From it emanated millions of lines—some white, some glistening, some sparkling, and still others dark. Some came out from the earth and stretched to some end point, only to take off again. Others came out and pooled back to a point where they joined others and soared off into the unknown. Others still just looped round.

"What you are seeing are the lines of all sentient beings that are on the planet. If we showed everything that we consider to be 'alive,' we wouldn't be able to see what is happening, so we have filtered this vision only to those things that as we say are sentient, either of your planet or those trying to influence it. We have also filtered out the lines of both Elgred and Charina, as they would obliterate all other lines. Those lines that you see that are either white or glisten in some way are those that are predominantly focused on adding what could be considered as positive good energy back into the universal all. Those that are grey and or much darker in color are those that focus on negative or evil energies."

Elji could see that there were far more light than dark, but as he watched he could see some of the lines beginning to grey a little, and the thought struck him that this was the influence of the evil overpowering the good. As the globe turned their

124

view did so with it, and he could see a cluster of very dark lines, twelve in all, arcing towards each other and a central point, though at one place he thought the beginning of one of these lines was beginning to lighten, and as he watched the light did seem to be spreading up the line.

"What you see here is the twelve of the Gouarong and their influence. You can see that where they touch the earth, a darkness spreads from there. They do all converge, and we assume that they do this where Framin is located, though when we have looked these lines shift and condense, and we have found it impossible to pinpoint the link. Framin has become adept at hiding his influence, and that is why we have such trouble finding him. But at least we have a place to start—we know the area to look. Of course, what we are seeing here is but the energy that comes from the earth. If we do this…." And the image changed. "We see the energies that feed into the earth and try to influence it."

Elji could see lines, some thick and strong and others much smaller and more numerous. Most of the lines were light in color, and stretched into the distance away from the earth. Some he thought he could almost glimpse the origins of, and at the ends he could see beings of immense power, beauty, and grace. But one was as dark as anything he had ever seen before. It jumped and darted around the face of the earth, never staying in one place for any length of time. He focused in on it and felt like he was being drawn in.

He entered the beam itself and was being sucked up away from the vision of the earth. His speed increased, as did the darkness. He was being pushed and pulled, and sped along the line. He was trapped—despair seeped into the very heart of his soul, and he began to scream a primeval scream. He thought he could see a huge black nothingness that he was hurtling towards. It was going to consume him, and as he sped toward it he could feel utter desolation and the end of everything he knew behind the blackness. Just at the moment he felt sure he was going to be consumed, something tugged on him and he crashed to the floor.

"Elji, Elji!" He could hear Dregar's voice calling him. "Elji, can you hear me?"

He was spent—he couldn't even open his eyes. It took all his energy to nod, and at that he passed into unconsciousness.

***

Elji came to and could see the others deep in conversation around the table. He couldn't tell what they were saying from where he was, but he could see that it was a frantic discussion.

He was lying on some kind of bed fashioned from the same material as the walls, but had a cushion on which his head rested. He sat up and could see Dregar pointing in his direction, though not facing him, and gesticulating to the others around the table. Elji tried to stand but there was no strength in his legs, so he sat back down on the edge of the makeshift bed.

Dregar turned at the noise and came across to him, followed by Amaran.

"Elji, how do you feel?" asked Amaran. "Do you know where you are?"

Elji nodded his head. "What happened? I was being swept up into some kind of dark hole. It felt as though it was devoid of everything, and was so all-consuming I could almost taste it."

"We don't know," said Dregar. "We have never, in all the time we have been dealing with the essence, either seen anyone interact in the way you did with a universal line, or seen anything have such control over what was occurring, In real terms, we were not even interacting, as we are removed twice from the reality of what is occurring on Earth. This is very worrying indeed, and it has opened up something that as far as we are concerned has never been experienced before." He looked very concerned. "What can you tell us about what happened more than you already have? We could not experience what you did, as it seems it was personal to only you, which in and of itself is most disconcerting. We could feel you were being taken from us, though, and I think if I had not intervened we may well have lost you to something we know nothing of."

"I'm not sure," said Elji. "I remember seeing the line reaching down to the earth. I was drawn into it and was being sucked up along its path. I could see complete and utter darkness, and what I can only describe as nothingness. Yet at the same time there was some kind of face, some kind of something beyond what I thought was nothing. I felt I was being consumed by it, and then I heard you call."

Dregar looked at Amaran. "There is nothing good in this. This is something that none of us have ever seen. I think we need to get this information to Elgred, and see if he knows anything about it. One thing that we do seem to have confirmed in all of this is that as far as we can see, Framin is influencing what is happening, and that perhaps something is influencing him. I guess we also know that Elji is much more important to us than we first realized. You, Amaran, must continue to find out what you can on what Framin seems to be doing and feed the information to me. Elji and I will go back to see Elgred."

"Just one more thing," said Elji. "I have only just remembered, just as I heard you call I saw what I can only describe as a very bright spec of light following me, though as you called it sped away and headed back to Earth. Time seemed to slow, and I saw it return to somewhere way in the north, above Mehem, to a great mountain range. Yes, yes…I am sure of it now. As it was happening I thought it just my mind, but I am sure I saw it."

"That is indeed something else that is strange," said Amaran. "We will see if we can make sense of that as well. Dregar, there may be something here that threatens to destabilize everything we know. Talk to Elgred — we will feed you what we can, but I would ask that you return the favor."

"Yes, I will certainly do that," said Dregar. "Can I suggest that you also speak to the Harood? You know they share this watch with us, and they are tasked with tracking Framin's influence on the earth. Elgred did ask that I go and speak with them again, but I think I can leave it up to you. Let me know what they think and say."

CHAPTER 17
THE FINDING OF ICHANCHA.

Cloin and Naimer began to walk up a path that was the beginning of the range of mountains that rose before them. They had wandered down the path as it wound around the foot of the mountain for a few hours since they had come to this place, and they were here based on the information they had been given by Elgred. Now it looked like it would start its ascent in earnest.

"Do you think we should just transport ourselves up to the top?" asked Naimer.

Cloin shook his head. "No. We don't know what we are looking for, and we don't know precisely where we may find it. So I think it best we make this part of the journey on foot. We could do with some serious exercise." He smiled at his sister, and they began the climb.

The path switched back and forth across the face of the mountain, and became steeper with every switch. Every now and then they came across steps cut into the face, and the path narrowed after each set. Soon they were facing a climb that could no longer be considered as following a path, and was just a hint of a way upwards.

Cloin looked down, and was encouraged to see they had come so far. But when he turned back and they made the top of one more crest, he realized that the distance they had come was a fraction of the total ascent. The mountain towered above them. It was getting colder too. He began to think that his sister had had the right idea after all. Still, there was no point in thinking about it, so he put his head own and carried on.

They climbed for hours, and as they got higher the air became thinner and the climb more difficult. As they made their way past one more switch in the climb, they came to a small plateau and stopped to rest.

"I think we should stay here for a while. Till we round the next rise, we have no idea how much further there is for us to go. If we stay here I can construct us a barrier against the cold, and we can recover a bit." Naimer did so without waiting for an answer.

They had been resting for no more than five minutes when they hear a cry, a screech. They both looked up and could see circling above them a large bird of some kind. It was getting lower and lower and was heading their way. Very soon it landed on the ledge with them, and tilted its head as if it were studying them. It hopped from side to side, and from one leg to the next, tilted its head, and looked again. It was huge, three or four times bigger than they had expected it to be from seeing it in the air. In fact, it was so big that it looked like it could carry either one of them away, if not both at the same time. It turned, and with one beat of its wings swept away from the ledge.

"What was that, do you think? I have never heard of a bird that large before. And it was strange," said Cloin. "I always thought eagles, if that's what it was, were solitary birds. It was as if it had come to have a look at us."

Unsure of what else to do, they sat back down to rest again.

Within a couple of minutes they heard the screech again, and could see the bird circling and heading towards them. Cloin was nervous, not sure what to make of this at all, and he just hoped that the thing hadn't decided they might make good food. They watched as the bird came closer and landed on the ledge.

From its back jumped a young woman. She was small in stature, and had hair the color of snow. It hung down her back to her knees, and was pulled tightly from her head, braided along its length. Her face was nearly as white as her hair, and her eyes were ice blue. The most striking thing about her was that, though her pupils were blue, the rest of her eyes, the sclera and the whites of her eyes, were black, as black as either of them had seen. So black it made her eyes almost shine from her face.

She smiled at them. "Hello. You are a long way up. I never get any visitors up here." As she came closer, it was clear that in fact she was more a young girl than a young woman.

Naimer dropped her weather protective shield and stepped forward. The great bird bristled, reared up, and shrieked.

"Shush," said the girl, and she looked at it. The bird tilted its head again as if listening, and settled back, satisfied that for now nothing more was needed. "I am sorry," the girl said. "As I said, we don't get anyone that comes up here, and she is nervous."

"She?" said Naimer. "With her size, I would have thought it a male. It's the biggest bird we have ever seen. Bigger than some of our horses."

"Horses?" the girl said, and seemed to think. "I have never

seen a horse."

Naimer stepped forward again. "I am Naimer, and this is my brother Cloin. I think we have come looking for you."

"For me?" said the girl. "Why would you be looking for me? I live here by myself with the eaglion—well, that's what I call them—and I have never been anywhere but here. Though I do watch—I watch everything. I love watching."

Cloin thought that eaglion was a good name for the bird. Halfway between an eagle and a lion was exactly how he saw it. He was still very unsure that they were safe as long as the bird was close by.

"We think," said Cloin, "that you may know something that might be able to help us. There is a man we know, who said we should come and try to find you and talk to you. Would you like us to tell you what we know, and how we think you might be able to help us?"

"Well, I have never met any real people before," she said. "So yes, I would like to hear what you have to say. Wait here." With that, she leapt onto the back of the bird and off the edge of the mountain. With two giant sweeps of the bird's wings she was up and gone.

Naimer and Cloin were left confused and a little dazed by the confrontation.

"Do you think that could be her?" asked Cloin.

"I don't know," said Naimer. "But she says she is alone, and has never met anyone before. Elgred did say that he expected she would not know who she was, and if she was alive she may not know what she was doing. She did say as well that she liked to watch. That makes me wonder if somehow or other she is tuned to the universal lines and is watching what is happening. How else might she be able to speak if not by watching people?

132

I don't think we have any choice but to see what unfolds. I just hope that whatever it is doesn't take us too long. We know that soon the Jalaria and Bremen and Saloora will try and destabilize what Framin does. If it is her and we can find out anything, it may help. I really don't know, but I think we should stay and find out."

As she finished speaking they heard a noise above them, and this time three of the giant eaglion were heading their way. The girl landed first and jumped down. "I stay some distance from here, so I have brought some friends to help take you there. Just sit behind their heads at the top of their necks — you will be quite safe."

There was not enough room on the ledge for all the eaglion, so the girl took off again and another of the birds landed.

"You first," said Cloin, and Naimer looked at him as if to say "why me?" But she climbed on anyway. No sooner had she gotten on than the eaglion leapt away. The third one landed and Cloin climbed on.

They soared and swooped up to the top of the mountain range and above, and headed further inland over sharp, snow covered peaks. The ride was exhilarating, and Cloin found himself beginning to enjoy the experience. As if by some silent communication, all three birds tucked in their wings and headed down with prodigious speed, straight for the top of a mountain. At the very last second they again spread their wings, swooped up over a ragged top, and landed on an open flat plain, not very big but big enough. In the center of the plain stood a solitary building — an old monastery, tiny and looking like it had been battered by the elements for a long time.

They all jumped down.

"This is where I stay," the girl said. "Do you want to go

inside?"

If they'd thought it was cold on the face of the mountain, up here the wind ripped into their skin and was trying to freeze their blood.

"Yes, please," said Naimer, and they headed off in the direction of the building.

Once inside it was a little warmer, if only for the fact that the walls were a barrier against the wind, but it was still bitterly cold. Naimer thought, though, that to make them more comfortable she should erect her barrier around the building, and so she did.

The girl's head shot up. "What did you do? What have you done?"

"What do you mean?" asked Naimer.

"You've done something. I felt it, and I can't feel the wind anymore. How have you done that?"

"Would you like me to take it away again?" asked Naimer.

"Wait," said the girl, and she sat down crossed legged in the center of the room. "Yes please," she said.

Naimer took the barrier away and the wind rushed back into the building. The girl looked up at her, and within seconds Naimer felt the barrier go back up.

"Interesting," they both said at once. The girl laughed, and Naimer laughed with her.

"I never knew that was possible," said the girl. "Not that I need the shelter — I am used to the wind and cold, but it is very interesting. Can you show me more?"

"There is a lot that my sister can show you," said Cloin. "But first we would like to know about you and what you are doing here. Could you tell us?"

"I have always been here," said the girl. "What a strange

question — I just am here. The eaglion bring me food, and there is a well behind this building. I sit at the edge of the flat here, and I watch and I listen. I have never actually met any other person before you two, but I have watched thousands and I listen to thousands more, and I see what they do. I am not sure why, but it seems to me that it is just what I am supposed to do. I like to watch and listen."

"So as you watch and you listen, have you seen anything that you think is strange?" asked Naimer.

"What do you mean strange?" asked the girl. "I watch the people. They just do things, and I watch them do it."

"OK, and what do you feel about some of the things you see them do?" asked Naimer.

"Feel?" She said. "I don't feel anything — they just do them."

Naimer turned to Cloin. "This is going to be difficult, and could take quite some time. I think we are going to have to discuss the nature of good and bad, and see what we can uncover by what she tells us." She turned back to the girl. "Would you like me to tell you of some things?"

"Tell me some things?" The girl asked. "Why don't you just let me see?"

At that Naimer felt the girl plunge into her mind, and it felt like she was sucking the information from her head — she was ravaging her mind.

"Stop!" Naimer screamed. "Stop!"

The feeling stopped, and the girl ran from the building.

Cloin looked at Naimer, who was on her knees, as if energy had been drained from her. Blood was dripping from her nose, and her eyes looked red, as if they had been bleeding on the inside.

"Are you OK?" he asked.

135

"Yes...," she gasped. "You had better follow her."

***

Cloin ran out the building after the girl.

He moved around the building to see if he could see the girl at the edge of the plateau, but as he rounded the corner she was there, huddled up against the wall of the building, scrunched into a ball. He went across to her and put his hand on her shoulder, and she jerked her head up.

Her eyes held his. The blackness of them bored into him, like they were burning a tunnel through his skull and into his brain. He couldn't stop her raiding his memories, and whatever else he had in his head. If felt like a worm was eating through his brain.

I Ie used all his mental strength and closed off his mind. She twisted away from him and stared at him. As she did he felt a wind behind him, and turned just in time to see one of the huge birds bearing down on him. He fell to the ground and rolled, pulling the sword from his back as he did so. As the huge bird swooped, he ran his sword along the underside of the creature, from head to tail, and it fell in front of him in a heap, blood and internal organs spilling everywhere.

The girl screamed, and again it brought him to his knees, but from the corner of his vision he saw his sister. He could see she was saying something.

He felt the presence of someone, and as he turned he saw Elgred and Charina. They both clapped their hands in unison, and the girl fell to the ground and the noise stopped.

His sister was there on her knees, blood still spilling from her nose. They both looked up at Elgred and tried to speak, but couldn't seem to find the strength.

"It's OK," said Elgred. "We have got this now. Charina and

ELJI AND THE GALRASS

I will take it from here. Let's all get back to Mehem, and from there we can decide what to do."

The wind disappeared and they were all back in the warmth of Mehem.

Cloin was finding it more and more difficult to try and concentrate on what was happening, He still felt as though there was some kind of a worm trying to bore itself into his skull and get at his brain.

"Elgred," he said. "Can you help me? I am not sure how much longer I can keep whatever it is that it trying to get inside my head out, and I get the distinct impression once it's in that may well be my undoing."

"I am sorry," Elgred said. "I had thought if the girl was unconscious she would not be able to hold her thoughts. Let me see what I can do."

He sat next to the girl and held her head in his hands. At once Cloin felt the pressure ease, and he could see that Naimer looked more at ease too.

Elgred let go of the girl and turned back to them. "We should be OK now." he said. "I have blocked us off from everything. I have severed all lines with any other living entity we know."

As he spoke the girl opened her eyes and looked at them all. "You dare," came an unknown voice from the girl, "to question my hold on everything?" At that a blackness sped towards them.

Elgred and Charina shifted everything in time and space, moving Cloin and Naimer away from the situation, and moving the girl and the other entity into an eternal loop of time and space. They constructed it so it was continually circling, like it was playing the same moment in time over and over again.

"That ought to hold whatever it is," said Charina, but

as she spoke the blackness that had approached reached out somehow, and Charina was pulled into the loop.

Elgred looked and smiled. "Well, that went better than we thought. Charina will now deal with what we know. It seems to me you found Ichancha!"

"You think that that is her?" asked Naimer. "And what has happened to Charina? Is she OK?"

"Yes, we do think that is her," said Elgred. "And Charina is fine. While you were away Dregar and Elji came back to see us. They had been to Dreger's home world, and while there had witnessed what we have just seen here. I think. I have spoken about this before, the black hole. Something that seems to have been created by the universe itself without our knowledge or interference. But what is different this time is that Elji thinks he saw a presence behind the blackness. Charina has gone to see what she can find. She will be back. We suspect it is something that is manipulating Framin, and has always manipulated him. We also think it is why Ichancha left us. We think that she could see what was happening, so she went to watch this 'thing,' whatever it is, all this time, trying to learn what its purpose is and what it does. The fact that we have the girl now means that we may begin to unravel this at last. We are not going to get to the bottom of this in time to help us with the immediate crisis, so we will take our time and learn what we can. I am sure it will play some important part before we are fully through with this planet's evolution, but for now Charina will watch, and if needed, we will be able to influence what happens in our favor."

Chapter 18
The home of the galrass

The vast desert of the Longraham stretched out before them. The heat beat down with an intensity that Elji had only ever felt near the forge of the blacksmith in his village. When he looked in the distance he could see the heat shimmering on the sand. It made it look like water was floating in small pools and lakes.

Sparse desert plants were dotted around, covered in spikes, but also soft looking. Dregar told him that these type of plants sucked up water when they could, and held it in the stems to use when it was needed. Some of the plants had become dislodged, and tumbled along the sand at a slow, stilting pace.

The sand itself had drifted into huge dunes, and they looked like massive yellow/brown waves on an ocean. The slight wind seemed to sift the tops of the dunes, and sand tumbled down one side or the other, making the dunes seem like they were moving.

Elji was mesmerized by the sight.

Dregar had brought them to this planet because he said that

the Kuwali that lived here were the makers of his galrass. He said they had the ability to create things of majestic complexity, and as such they needed to talk to them about his galrass.

If indeed this race had made his stone, then they would be able to teach him what it was and how best to utilize it.

Since they had come an hour or so ago they had not seen anything but sand. Dregar said they were to wait for dusk, then they could move. Watching the sand and feeling the heat, he was happy to be as motionless as possible.

"This world, in your terms of time, is fairly old," said Dregar. "And its people have been around for a very long time. They chose many thousands of years ago to stay on their world, and not be directly involved in the growth of the universe and the life within it, wanting only to concern themselves with the peace of their own planet. They have indeed made a very good job of it. As far as any of us know, there has never been any conflict here; each person has total respect for the other. They are a simple people who live mainly near the coast. They fish, and they herd a kind of sheep/goat. They don't build great cities, and don't seem to have the need to conquer one another. They are a friendly people, and always happy to talk and eat.

"The black stone that your galrass is made of is found in plentiful supply in seams that start in the oceans here, and it has a property that enables the shaman of these people to interact with and manipulate the universal essence into making copies of the current magnitude of the universe."

"What do we hope to do by coming here?" asked Elji. "Can these people help us at all?"

"Because they made the galrass that you own, they will be able to instruct you in the way it ought to be used, and how you can utilize it to help others. As I said to you before, a galrass doesn't usually end up in the hands of someone who is not a scholar. There are no more than a dozen such things in the whole universe, and all of the rest of them reside here. These people don't use them to manipulate the timelines or interfere in the passage of all things, but they do, when asked from time to time, give a galrass to be used in time of need. I suspect that this is what has happened and why you have your hands on one. They — and by that I mean the galrass — tend only to work for certain people, almost like they can feel the person that is trying to manipulate them. I am almost certain that if I tried to use your galrass, very little would happen."

"So why do they make them if they don't do anything with them?" asked Elji.

"Because they believe that they hold the true power of harmony, and as a race of people they are very involved in creating harmony. By creating copies of the universe in different stages, they are storing that harmony." Dregar smiled.

Elji hunkered down again to wait, and he became lost in thought. "There is something I kept meaning to ask you, Dregar. Why do you carry and use your stick? I mean, I am fairly sure that your manipulation of the essence doesn't rely on your stick, yet whenever we move anywhere you always brandish it in a pattern of some kind."

"Ahh," laughed Dregar. "You noticed that, did you? Now there's a story. Let's wait till we meet the people, and I will have the greatest of pleasure in telling you that story."

"Why, if as you say, these people live near the coast, are we waiting in the middle of all this sand?" asked Elji.

"Because all is not as it seems, and we must wait for dusk."

The sun began to tilt low in the sky and the air had bit by bit become cooler and less searing to breathe, although it was still hot by any standard. As it slowly descended it cast a deep red glow across the sand, making the desert come alive in a different way.

Elji could see small plants start to push through the sand and sprout luminescent flowers. It happened very quickly and filled up his vision. They were everywhere, and the effect was transformational and beautiful.

As he looked out across the expanse of light, he saw a group of people cresting one of the great dunes. As they walked, they disturbed the flowers and they floated up into the air, causing a dance of luminosity that followed them as they walked. Soon they were standing before Elji and Dregar.

"Welcome, friends," said a man at the front of the group. All the men were wearing what could be described as long robes. Light in color and in material, they were floating around the bodies of the people. On their heads they wore more of the same cloth, held to their heads by a band of rope that was just heavy enough to keep the headdress in place, it cascaded down as if they had long hair. There were many colors, some red, most white, but some checked with red and white. The women wore the same cloth, though it was draped across them in a different fashion and was much shorter, falling just below the waist and clasped in the front just below the breast. Their hair was mainly black and adorned with mother of pearl and gold. They were alluring in the extreme.

"Welcome to the Kuwali," the man said again, sweeping his arm around.

Dregar smiled and embraced the man, kissing him on each cheek. "Thank you, Shamshar. It's good to see you again. Peace be upon you."

"Ahh Dregar, my friend. Peace be upon you also. Who is

this you have with you?" He asked. "Oh, never mind that. Let's go and get settled, and you can tell us why you come to visit."

He turned, and they all made their way across the top of the dune. As they crested the top Elji could see that in front of them was a settlement made up of low structures, all topped with some kind of thick brown cloth draped across long thick poles. The sides were covered in much more colorful cloth, and many sides were pulled back to reveal the interiors and let in whatever breeze was available.

As he looked closer he could see that the whole settlement was lit by some kind of fauna that emitted the same luminescent light as the flowers had done in the desert, and beyond the structures themselves he could see the sea. It was calm, not a ripple to be seen on the surface, and a light came from below the water, turning it into a mercurial pool. The sun hung just above the horizon, mixing a shade of red with the silver of the water.

As he looked he could see small spouts of water being emitted here and there, their colors beautiful to behold in blues, oranges, yellows, and purples. As they fell back to the water he thought he could hear a tinkling sound. He stopped walking to watch.

"They are the alhitan," said a voice beside him, and he turned to look.

Standing next to him was a young woman whose beauty, in Elji's opinion, surpassed even that of Charina and Saloora. She was no taller than him, and had jet black hair that cascaded down her back. Her skin was the color of light coffee, and in the lights that were around it was glistening and sparkling as if alive. She wore the same simple cloth shift, which barely seemed to cover anything at all, but just enough to be alluring in its arrangement. Her face was regal in appearance—small, petite, the proportions of which, to his mind, were perfect. Her lips were a kind of deep red verging on brown, and looked to be so soft. In short, he was mesmerized.

"My name is Talisha," she said, and smiled at him. "The alhitan come every night and join in the beauty of our planet. Later we will hear them sing."

Elji could not speak. He just nodded and continued to stare at the woman.

"Are you always this quiet?"

"Well…err…well…. No," he spluttered, and she laughed, a magical light sound that seeped into him.

She reached down and took his hand, and faced him square on. "Let me try again," she said. "I am Talisha, daughter of the tribal father, Shamshar, princess of the silver sea, and I welcome you to our land."

Elji spluttered again. "Errr…I am Elji, of the village Nebaril," he managed to get out.

"Welcome, Elji, Peace be upon you," she said, and still holding his hand she turned and led them towards the settlement. "These," she told him, pointing at the settlement, "are called beits—it means tent in your language."

Elji could feel his heart racing as they walked, and his palms had become sweaty. He felt like he should pull his hand away and wipe it, but he didn't want to let go. The feeling of her hand in his was intense and filled his whole being. So they walked hand in hand, following the others.

Dregar looked back at them and laughed, shook his head, and turned back to talk to Shamshar.

As they walked towards the central beit they passed many people, all sitting, either outside or in the open sided beits.

Fires were burning in many places, though the heat from them wasn't needed. Indeed, they didn't seem to be giving off much heat, and the flames were a light blue color that cascaded up into the sky, adding to the atmosphere.

"These places where the people sit," said Talisha, "are called diwaniya. They are made specifically for people to meet and talk of family, of business, and of love and peace."

They reached the central beit and Talisha led him to a cushion by a central fire and sat down next to him. Elji was lost in sensations, all of them calming and all of them peaceful. At once he felt at home and at peace.

As he sat the men rose from the cushions and walked out, only to return in a matter of less than a minute carrying huge silver platters covered in food. They placed them around the guests. Then the women rose and came back carrying small glass cups and small tea pots called dallahs. They placed them on the ground and sat again.

Shamshar stood once more and said, "Be still, listen from within. Feel your purpose.

"Embrace the energy, the power, the meaning. Tune your whole to that. Receive it, just be. Understanding, truth, flows from there. Become all you can. Unleash love. The universal soul knows the way. Believe it, join it. Awaken. Now let us eat and talk away our cares, and speak of things only related to love." And he sat again.

Elji looked in front of him at the food, and then round the beit. People were taking flat bread and spooning rice, meat, and vegetables onto it, using it almost as a plate and using more bread to eat it with. There were also smaller plates filled with pastes and mixes, all of which he watched people dip their bread into. He did the same.

People were moving around, squatting by the food, picking some up, eating, talking, and moving again. The effect was that everyone talked to each other. Soon laughter was the loudest sound. As they walked around and sat, they touched each other without fear of rejection; many embraced and kissed cheek to cheek. Children had come in from somewhere, and were sitting around in people's laps talking and singing.

Someone started clapping in a rhythm. Others joined in with an offbeat clapping, and yet others started to sing. The women interjected with voices and notes of their own. It was mesmeric, and Elji was transported across the water. He could see the alhitan; they were whale type creatures and were spouting water, but as they did so, basic universal tones were also coming from their spouts. He was transported again by the sound. He spiraled into the universe, swimming through the galaxies and stars, twisting and turning slowly. He felt in perfect harmony with all creation.

The singing stopped and he came back. Everyone was silent for a moment, and then the talking and laughter began again.

He thought that if he never experienced anything again in his life, what he had just experienced was sufficient to have made his life worthwhile. He was at peace. This, he thought, must be what Dregar had been speaking of. These people knew their place in the universe, and how kindness and love could lead to an existence that was all it needed to be.

Talisha turned to Elji and took his hand. "Come with me," she said. They got up and she led him away from everyone, and towards the edge of the sea. "Take off your shoes," she said.

He did, and noticed she was bare footed. They walked hand in hand right at the edge of the water, which was gently lapping at their feet and was warm, and it soothed him even

146

more than he already was. He was content to just walk. As they walked the laughter got more and more distant, and a silence descended on them both. When Elji turned he could no longer see the beits.

"Have we rounded a cove or something?" Elji asked. "I didn't realize we had been walking so long."

"No, we have not," said Talisha. "But our place at this time in the universe is just for you and me, so everything else has faded, though of course it is still there. There is something I would like to show you. It's not far now."

He didn't mind. He was content, as content as he had ever been.

Talisha stopped in front of an opening that led into one of the large dunes that were along the edge of the shore. He looked at her.

"We need to go in here," she said, and led him in.

The entrance was lit by the same florescent light, and it was wide enough for them to walk side by side easily. It was going up at a steady angle, though how that was possible he wasn't sure, as they would have walked right back out of the top of the dune. But upwards it went. They reached a kind of room made from the same stone as his galrass. As he looked around he could see the interlaced lines, and could see that they were alive, as were the lines in his galrass.

"This," said Talisha, "is where we fashion the galrass. Each one we make captures the essence of the universe precisely at the time it is fashioned. But as the universe expands and changes, so does the content of this room and the content of the galrass. We do not make a galrass unless it is necessary, as it gives access to the whole universe at will. We are guided by this room. It seems to tell us when we should make one and who it is for, though it does not tell us the reason we make one for someone. You, I know, have one. We sent it to your world for you to find. This means that in the scheme of the universe, you have something that it needs, and something that will help to shape what is to come. You, Elji, have been chosen. You have some gift we do not know of, but here is where you will find the true purpose of your choosing.

"I am going to leave you here, and I want you to listen and feel what is being shown to you. When you come from this room you will never be the same again. You will learn things you will not want to know. You will learn the span of your life. You will learn the challenge you face, and you will learn your part in it all. You may not like what you are shown, but remember, you can choose to reject the path if you want to. The choices will be laid out for you. I will be here waiting when you return."

With that, Elji felt his whole existence spin away from him.

CHAPTER 19
UNRAVELLING

The armies of the Jalaria had assembled outside the ten cities they were to attack. The Drendrak had used their graithes and had created bridges through the universal essence to places far enough away from each of the cities that they would not be seen till it was time, and they had gotten their armies through without mishap. Sure, there had been a few skirmishes along the way, but nothing that they had not been able to contain.

Though the armies were spread over continents, the Drendrak kept in close contact via their graithes. This way the attacks could be coordinated and create as much chaos as possible so that Framin would be unable to assist in any one place. The hope was that their attacks on the cities would distract Framin enough to allow Bremen and Saloora time to discover what was happening with the universal lines and portals, and give them enough time to disrupt them and then pass on information on how to deal with them.

Harther stood at the edge of the temperate forest, where his army was dispersed just outside the city of Bengradi. Santarish ruled the city, and even from Harther's vantage point he could see it was in a state of disrepair. He didn't think for one minute, though, that the army that defended Bengradi would be a pushover, and he had no doubt the battle would be fierce.

The call to attack would come soon, and he had decided earlier in the day to get some of his men into the city to ensure that as much chaos as possible was created when they got the word. He'd always hated this bit, the waiting—he was a fighter... he liked fighting. It was when he felt most comfortable; well, either that or drinking, and what came along with drinking. He was, though, a seasoned warrior and he knew his business. He wouldn't fail, and soon enough his liking for fighting would be satisfied.

The call came. Harther signaled and his men started to move forward towards the edge of the city. He had decided that they would use as much stealth as possible, as his men numbered around only two-hundred. It didn't worry him, though; he had taken much larger cities than this before with such a number of men.

The men stayed low, using as much cover as possible. He hoped that those he had sent to the city earlier in the day had managed to dispense of any guards that may be watching the approaches—he was sure they had. They had chosen a gate into the city that looked like it was the least used, and indeed, for the last hour or so he had seen no one coming or going. That served him well.

***

Bremen, Saloora, and Florin had moved into a building close to the palace. Florin and his men used the building on a daily basis to interact with those in the palace, so being there would not arouse much suspicion now.

150

Jalad had asked for a meeting with the captain of the guard for the palace, on the pretense that he had uncovered some plot in the city that he thought the captain should know about. This would be enough for him to get Bremen and Saloora into the palace.

"Once we are in you will be on your own." said Jalad. "Hopefully while we are there the men will start creating the diversions we discussed around the city, and the chaos should allow you to move around the palace without arousing too much suspicion. OK, let's go."

They set off. It was dark in the palace, and there didn't seem to be many people anywhere.

"Something has changed," said Jalad. "While this was always a gloomy sort of place of late, it did have some life in it, and it certainly didn't feel as oppressive as it does now."

They came to the end of a corridor and Jalad knocked on a door. "Come," said a voice, and they pushed open the door.

The captain was seated behind a desk in a room that could only be called dingy. Standing behind him were three men who were covered in scars from battle. They looked hard, with eyes like stone that didn't flicker as they looked at Jalad.

"What do you want?" the captain asked. "I hear you have some news of trouble for me?"

"Yes," said Jalad. "A few nights ago down near the docks, we heard some men talking and plotting to get down to the armory and into the passages below the city. What was interesting was that they had some bales with them that seemed to be made of more than just hay or straw. They were tightly bound and had some kind of fuse hanging out. They were huge. I can only guess that they were some kind of explosive. I couldn't come and tell you straight away as they made their way across the lake, so we thought it best to follow them. They picked up more men in the next town along the coast, and more bales, then came back. We followed them then to the building that used to be the tannery at the east end of the palace. As you know, that building hasn't been used for years. As I say, we thought you should know."

As they were speaking a series of loud rumblings could be heard from outside.

The captain and his men jumped up. "Get out!" he said. "Make your way back to the city, and if you see anything on the way deal with it."

They all left the room in a hurry.

Once through the door Bremen and Saloora turned back and headed down a different corridor that they thought would lead them deeper into the palace itself.

Jalad followed the captain and his guards out of the palace. As they exited the main entrance to the palace, it was clear that there was smoke coming from the city itself.

"You…," said the captain. "Get your men and help us round up anyone that seems suspicious, and bring them back here." He turned.

As he did, Jalad's men that were waiting for him outside engaged the captain and his three guards. In no time they were lying in pools of blood on the ground, but more men were issuing from the door and the fight was joined in earnest.

An alarm could be heard from a garrison close to the palace, and men ran from all directions. Confusion reigned. Men engaged each other at every corner, and screams could be heard down every street. Jalad had made the decision to position archers at strategic junctions within the city, and while his men were outnumbered, a plan was in place, and they were cutting down the palace guards with ease.

***

Bremen and Saloora came to a junction in the corridor and were left with a decision to go right or left. They stopped and took stock. Now that they were on their own they could see that the walls of the palace were very dark, as if covered in some kind of matter that wanted to suck the life force from them.

"We must be close," said Bremen. "Something here is feeding the walls and the very air with despair and hatred. It's as if they are living and breathing themselves. It seems to be worse this way. Let's go."

As they walked, a sound was emanating from the end of the corridor they were in and the air was getting thicker with the feeling of death. They entered a room at the end and stopped short. It was huge, its proportions at odds with everything. It was much bigger than could possibly be accommodated in the palace building.

There were steps down to a level below them, and some distance away they could see, in the center of the room, a device much like the one Bremen had in his quadrangle. Lines were reaching into and coming from a central source, but these lines were thick and black. Around the central device were huge deep pits filled with cages that held hundreds of women, children, and old men. The despair in the room was so real that it seemed to be coloring the air.

Standing by the device in the center was Kahilja. Even at this distance his huge bronze body glimmered, and the power he held could be seen. His hands were immersed in the black lines, and he was feeding them with the despair from the prisoners they held in the room.

"We have to get to him," said Bremen, "and hope that the attacks on the other cities make him more vulnerable."

153

The rest of the Jalaria had started their assaults on each of the cities that had been chosen. Each attack had been planned and orchestrated to get the Drendrak as close to each universal portal as possible. Once this was achieved, they would all join together and wrestle the control away from the Gouarong, free each of the cities, and begin the long process of bringing truth and hope back to the people.

***

Harther and his men had been battling to accomplish this as quickly as they could. Their attack had surprised the city, and at first they had made good progress towards the main palace, where the Drendrak had said the portal would be. Now, however, the defense was becoming more organized, and as they closed in the men they were facing were a different caliber of fighter, consumed with an ability to throw themselves into the fight with no regard for their lives.

Harther and his men were on the very street that the palace was on and had it surrounded. Behind them there was some resistance from the general populace, but mainly they were all hiding and keeping out of the way. He was a little worried— it was a bit of a stalemate, and he needed something that would give his men another push. He turned and spoke to his Drendrak, Vladoon, his brother in battle.

"Is there anything you can do to cause some kind of distraction that may make this final push happen a little more quickly?"

With that Vladoon smiled, and said "Always," then disappeared.

"Bloody Drendrak," said Harther, to no one in particular. "Just disappearing as they like."

No sooner had he finished speaking then men started

running out of the palace in numbers. He could hear a roar from inside the palace that shook the very ground he was standing on. His men wasted no time, and rushed into battle with those fleeing the palace. It was a slaughter. Harther's archers were bringing down the fleeing men in numbers, and those that made it past the arrows were being taken care of by the rest of the men. It was an orchestrated blood bath.

Harther looked round and Vladoon was back by his side. "Well, that seemed to work," he said. "What did you do?"

"I just made them think that something inside the palace was a lot worse than what was on the outside." He smiled and laughed, raised his sword, gave out a battle cry, and said, "Come on, let's finish this."

He and Harther raised another cry together and ran towards the building. The rest of his men saw this, and letting out battle cries of their own rushed headlong into the melee.

***

Bremen and Saloora had managed to work their way round to where Kahilja stood. The people that were being held in the cages did not seem to notice them at all as they passed, and all that were alive were in a state that could only be called trancelike. In each cage there were many bodies that looked like they'd had the life sucked out of them — they were no more than piles of bone and skin.

Kahilja was motionless, and his body seemed to course with the energies coming from the device. His eyes were absent and black. His head was tilted upwards and his mouth was stuck in a scream, though no sound was coming out.

Bremen approached him from behind and reached out with his hand to place it on his shoulder. As he touched his skin he became rigid and fixed also. Saloora could see that his face

155

was in a grimace that showed a state of pain she had not seen before. He was breathing hard, and she could tell that he was struggling, even with all his knowledge, to hold on. She acted.

Moving to a place she could get a good strike, Saloora removed a sword from her back and sliced through both of Kahilja's arms just above the wrists. Bremen gasped in a large gulp of air. The whole of the room became still in an instant. The lines recessed back into the device, Kahilja fell to the ground, and as he did silence, complete silence, took hold.

"Get me to the device," Bremen said through gasps. "We need to reconnect with the essence. Otherwise I fear that Framin will feel this disruption and will be alerted."

She helped him stand above the device, where he closed his eyes and started to direct the lines of essence, connecting them with each other so that they looped away. One by one they disappeared from sight. Still black, still seeming to seethe with evil, but gone nonetheless.

Bremen collapsed.

***

Harther stopped and looked around. They had made great progress; the fighting had lessened, and they had been able to gain access to the palace and had fought their way into a central room. He turned to see where Vladoon was, and as he did he was hit from the side by a man that was as big as anyone he had seen in his life, bronze in color and rippled with muscle. He assumed it was Santarish. Vladoon had told him how they had fashioned themselves in the likeness of Framin, and had been given powers by him to do this.

All this sped through his mind as he was falling to the floor, and he could see Santarish bringing down his sword to end his life. It was deflected at the last moment, and Harther saw

156

Vladoon engaging with the giant of a man. Harther stood up and reached for the wall to get his balance. As he put his hand on the wall he could feel it was almost alive; it had a flesh like quality to it, and it was pulsating. He pushed off and attacked Santarish from behind. The man sprung out of the way with cat like reflexes that belied his size. Now both Vladoon and Harther faced him square on.

They watched him and began to separate from each other, never taking their eyes off him so that Santarish had to try and defend two sides. As they were moving apart, Santarish stiffened. A blade come through his stomach and he fell. Cloin stood behind him, with Naimer at his side.

"We thought you might need some help." Cloin smiled at them.

"I'm sure we could have coped with him, but many thanks for the help. It has shortened the ending," said Harther. "It is good to see you both. Have you come to help us finish off this thing?"

"We have been helping in the struggle in a different way, but we have finished that now. So we are going to help where we can. Vladoon, you need to get to where the lines are coming from and turn them back in on themselves so that they stop feeding malice outwards. We are going to go and help others in different cities. If we can turn them all back inwards, we may be able to get the balance back in favor of more pleasant things. Beware, though; there seems to be something more at play here than just Framin. I think our best plan is to coordinate every one of our Drendrak to assault the lines at the same time. Wait for the call from your brothers. We will go and see where we can help."

Cloin and Naimer disappeared as quickly as they had

appeared.

"OK," said Harther. "You go and take a look at this central portal, and I will ensure you are not disturbed."

***

Bremen regained his consciousness, and could see that Saloora was bent over him with a worried look on her face.

"I am OK," he said. "Something within the essence rushed at me when I started to move the lines back on to each other. It took me by surprise. It was very dark indeed, and filled with hopelessness and fear. We need to get this information to all the Drendrak so that they know what they face. Let me speak to Elgred — he can get the message out, and we can see what we must do next."

***

Bremen reached out and spoke to Elgred. *Something is at work here that I do not know about. I felt something new that I have not felt before. Let me give the experience to you, and you can reach the rest of the Drendrak and tell them what we plan.*

Yes, said Elgred. *I can do that. You are right, there is something else at play here that we have not anticipated. Charina and I know something about it, and Cloin and Naimer found what we think is the essence of Ichancha. She seems to be tangled up in this thing. Charina is trying to find out what she can. I don't think we will have time to unravel it all now as we try and turn this situation around, but the fact that we are aware does help us. Hopefully we can deal with what we face now, and then try and understand the true nature of what has been discovered. For now, I think your best course of action is to go to where we think Framin is. Once there, see what you can find out without him knowing. Others will come and join you, and we will see if we can undo this and tip the balance back in our favor. I will give the information to the Drendrak.*

158

***

Bethrod called for Tragarg. "Do you have any news for me? I must decide where to go to help the most."

"All battles are being fought and the Jalaria are winning. Our prior knowledge and the element of surprise has certainly worked in our favor. In two cities we already control the portals, and we are very close in the others. Once the Drendrak are all in place, we will make the final assault on the portals and try and turn the lines back to our advantage. Bremen has learned something, and Elgred has sent the message to all the Drendrak, so we now know what to expect. Bremen and Saloora have made their way to where we suspect Framin is, and soon Cloin and Naimer will join them there. Perhaps your best course of action is to go there and see how you might help. I suspect it will all come to a head at that place. If we can unseat Framin there, then we will have won control for now. If we can unravel what is behind it all we could put an end to it for good. I doubt, though, that we have the information and knowledge we need to do this. I have not heard from Elgred on anything else. I know that there were some others involved in this, but I don't know where they are or what hope of help we have from them. If you go I will come with you."

"No," said Bethrod. "We have already risked everything we have. When we come out of this we need people who are able to coordinate and manage the reintegration of all the cities and the people. You and the Drendrak are needed for this. I am a warrior, and my presence may tip the balance in our favor when we confront Framin, if indeed that happens. I already risk my children in this, and I need someone to stay here and help Kreanna. You are the closest thing to family we have. So I wish you to stay here, coordinate the Drendrak, and support

159

her if we do not return."

Bethrod made his way to join Bremen, Saloora, Cloin, and Naimer.

**

The room was dark and damp. Bremen and Saloora were waiting for the others, and Bremen had cloaked their presence so that Framin would not know they were there. The building was some distance from where Framin had taken up residence, but not too far, as it would take too long to get there. It was a rundown shack that had at some point or other been used to house livestock. The floor was covered in straw and mud, but in the light that they had they couldn't be sure it was indeed mud, and the smell suggested it may be something different.

There was a noise outside the hut and the door was being rattled. As it opened Bremen disguised them both. Cloin and Naimer walked in and looked around.

"They are not here," said Naimer.

"We are," said Saloora, and they appeared. "Bremen thought it best we were hidden in case it was an unwanted visitor."

"We did try and get to your precise location," said Cloin. "But Naimer couldn't find you."

"Yes, that would be for the same reason you couldn't see us," said Saloora. "Any way, we are here now."

At that someone else entered the building and they all spun around, ready to answer any danger.

"Good to see you are all on your toes," said Bethrod, and he came across and embraced his children. "And it is good to see you both again, still in one piece."

"We are fine," said Cloin. "It's been interesting so far, but we haven't been in that much danger — well, apart from almost being eaten by a huge bird/lion creature, and Naimer being attacked by an unknown entity, that is." He smiled at his father. "What do we know of how things are going?"

It was Saloora that answered. "We managed to get to the portal that was being used by Kahilja, and then made our way here."

"OK, that's good. So along with the fact that we control the portal used by Santarish, and the information we have gathered for the other Drendrak, we seem to be in fairly good shape," Bethrod added.

"If I understand what Elgred wants from us, it is to sit tight here till Elji and Dregar join us, wait for the rest of the Drendrak to be in place, and try and see if we can take hold of what Framin has here."

"I suppose, then, that for now we wait," said Bremen.

CHAPTER 20
FROM BOY TO MAN

He was floating in what appeared to be a sea of glistening lights, but he knew that it was a representation of the whole universe. As he floated he began to feel a sensation of movement. The lights started to drift past him and get faster and faster, and soon it was as if he was in a tunnel rushing toward an end.

He spun out of the end and felt himself in a void. He could hear and see nothing. He got the distinct feeling that he was the only living thing in his space.

Elji tried to orient himself in the space, but as there was nothing to do that against, it was a futile gesture. As he struggled he found his mind wandering back to his home village, and the woods where he had found the galrass. Suddenly he was looking at himself and his dog outside the wood. He could see Aker bounding off into the wood toward a light, and though he could not hear anything, he knew what he was saying and watched as he followed the dog.

As he looked to the wood he could see the light emitting from the galrass, but this time he could see lines extending into the sky and beyond.

"Any one of those lines could have been the possible future at that point," he heard a voice say. "By your actions at that point, you chose the possible future to go down."

Elji looked around — he still could not see anything other than the vision of himself following his dog. He looked down and he could see his feet were on the grass in the field, and he had some orientation. Beside him was a being he had never seen before. It shone with an intensity that was not so much bright as it was alive, and it had a quality that suggested it was made from the very fabric of everything around it. As he looked closer he could see at the center a version of his galrass. He was puzzled. How could his galrass be inside a being? He stared at it, and as he did so he plunged into it.

Again he was suspended in the sea of glistening lights. They began to move again and sped past him. Again he was ejected into the void. This time the vision of the field and the wood was different. He could see it was still the wood outside his village, but it was as if it had a disease. Everything was more subdued in color, and many of the trees had been felled or were rotting. He looked around and could see a man trudging through the field away from the wood and back to the village. He watched and his perspective changed.

He was outside his house, and the man walked up to the door and entered, Inside he could see an old woman lying on a bed, frail and spent. He realized the man was him, and that this was his mother. As he looked at her she faded, and in her place was his galrass again. As he looked he was transported back into the lights and the travelling started again. He was ejected into the void.

This time he expected to see his field and the woods, but

instead he was looking at a barren piece of land. People toiled in the land, bent and broken. He could see others at the edge of the field, walking with sticks and wielding whips to make sure the people worked. As he looked at the people in the field he saw his mother and brothers and other people from his village. He wanted to cry out to them and help them, and reached out for his mother, running towards her. As he ran he ended up in the lights and the journey began again.

Again and again the journey happened—each time a different vision, each time a different situation. Some were tragic to watch while some were visions of perfection and harmony, but he couldn't stay at any of them.

"OK, OK, I get it," he shouted. "There are unimaginable possible futures based on events and belief and actions."

Everything stopped and he was standing in a circle of light. All round him were beings of differing kinds, some describable, some not.

The voice came again. "Elji, you have two choices. You have been given an opportunity to become part of everything that you know, and help us guide and create the universe toward the light. In doing this you will be able to help those that you care about and the race that you belong to, but you will never be one of them again. You will become what you might consider immortal. This will mean that you will lose everything and everyone you know in time, and you will have to be concerned with much more than just your planet and your race. It will be painful and lonely, but the rewards can be great. The fact that you have been chosen to be here means that your part in this is important, and your participation may well tip the balance in the favor of good—and you may well be able to help those you love. Your sacrifice to watch everything you cherish die in the end could give them a better life than they could hope to have without your involvement.

"Or you can choose to return to where you were, and hope that others can influence the outcome and that the good within your race will win. You will be just a boy in a village. You will not remember anything that you have seen and done till now, but you will always know that there could be a better way, a better future. If you choose the first course we will give you knowledge that you can call on when needed. If you choose the second way, we will return you now."

Elji laughed. "In the short time since I discovered this stone, it seems to me that none of my life has been in my control. I have seen and done and learned more in this short space of time than I had done in all the time I lived in my village. I want to know more, but I wish more than anything to have some semblance of control over what is happening to me and be able to help those that I love. Though I have my family, I have no other relationships that I can say I would miss or regret if I outlived them."

"You are not considering that in actual fact, you will in the future forge more relationships and meet those that you fall in love with. I can tell you now that you do, in the future, have a family, and you will see all of them die. You are considering only that which you know now—you are not considering all that might be," said the voice.

"In the short time I have been involved in all of this, and from what I know, I think that I will take my chances with continuing to learn. If I have learned nothing but this, it is that, as you have shown me, there are immeasurable possible futures, and it may be that I can influence how this future turns out." He smiled. "Unless, of course, you are telling me that certain things are predetermined?"

"No, we are not suggesting that. But we are telling you that in all things, probability has its place, and based on all possible outcomes this must be weighed."

"I am ready, despite the probability, to take my chances. I will learn what I can and help all the people of my race. Even if it means personal loss and pain. As I see it, all things are part of the essence, and to lose someone is not the end—it is but part of a journey."

"This is why you have been chosen, Elji," said the voice. "The fact that your mind works this way and has a basic understanding of the concepts is the reason the galrass came to you. We will show you now what we think is necessary. It will take time, years as you know it. You will reside here, and you will return an older person than you are now. But the timeline on your world and the world of the Kuwali will not have changed. You will be where you are needed at the time you are needed. Do not worry on this."

Elji felt and heard again the change in his reality, and he slipped into the void again and began his learning.

Elji woke back in the room, where Talisha was standing where she had been when he had merged into the void. She looked at him and he looked at her. She smiled.

"I see you are no longer the boy you were."

Elji looked puzzled. "What do you mean? Can you see a physical difference? They told me it would take time, but I didn't suspect that I would actually change."

"Come with me," she said, and she took him to another room and stood him in front of what could only be described as a mirror, though it was constructed of a fluid substance like water. As he looked it cleared, and as it cleared it cycled through different images of him. It settled, and he tilted his head to one side and looked more closely.

Gone was the boy, and in his place was a young man in his mid-twenties. His face had changed into that of a man and not a boy. He had grown in stature, though he could still see himself in the image. He looked a little like his brothers—he was bigger and broader, though nowhere near the height they had attained. As he looked he felt that the biggest change was in his perception of what he saw. He saw someone confident and assured, someone with knowledge.

He laughed and turned to look back at Talisha. "I like it," he said, and she laughed with him.

"As do I, Elji. I think it's best we go back and see what Dregar has to say, and you can decide what you need to do next. Before we do that, though, there is one more thing I would like to take care of."

She took his hand and led him down the corridor to a door. They entered, and this one was different from the rooms he had seen so far. It was a sleeping quarter, and though it was part of what they had entered beneath the sand, it was open to the world. He could see the ocean, he could see the dunes, and he could see the sky and all that was in it.

"We have a tradition here," said Talisha. "When we meet someone we feel we know, then we are able, if we want to, to share all ourselves with them. Elji, I feel I know you. You are special, I can feel that, and I want to share myself with you now. Will you accept that sharing?"

As she spoke she came close to him and pulled herself into him. He noticed that whereas before they had been a similar size, he was now taller than her, He had also felt nervous and excited in her presence, but now felt confident and attracted.

He leaned down and kissed her. "It would be my pleasure," he said, and they gave in to the urges they both felt. His surroundings swam again, but this time he immersed himself in all the feelings he could, and they forged a connection that surprised them both.

He raised himself from the bed on his elbow and looked at her, and she looked at him and said, "I will come with you. Sometimes you know when something is meant to be and what you are supposed to do, and this is one of those times. I know now that my life is with you." She smiled.

Elji smiled back at her. "Then that means that already my life has changed for the better, and I consider myself one of the luckiest men alive."

She laughed. "I am sure it will not all be as pleasant as this moment, though I think we can share something that is truly worth sharing, and we will discover and create wonderful things together."

Elji smiled. "We will indeed. Now let's go and see what we must do." At that he all but leapt from the bed, laughing at himself. "I must remember that I am not as I used to be. It might take some getting used to." He leaned down and kissed her again. "Thank you, Talisha."

"There is no need to thank me. It is as it should be."

They made their way back towards the others.

CHAPTER 21
FRAMIN'S PORTALS

Framin could feel that his Gouarong were all in place. The despair and death that was coming from their portals was growing. He knew that the reach they had now would influence the local people in all the cities, and they would turn towards malice and greed.

He loved the potential this race provided—their instinct towards needing more made them easy to manipulate and use. He was certain that these people and this planet would enable him to reach his goal to gain back that which Elgred and the others had stripped from him. He was stronger now than he had been for millennia, and he could feel something in the essence that was feeding him, giving him the desire to continue. He was sure this was the universe telling him he was on the right path.

It didn't matter to him that over time he had left worlds desolate of any form of what could be considered reasonable life. He had plunged many into total darkness. One world he had managed to influence enough that they now helped him across the universe to wage war against all that was good. They had been especially malleable, and he was able to turn them into a race that waged war to try and devour other races. He missed them. Ichancha, before she disappeared, had managed to manipulate the essence enough that as a race, they could no longer surge across worlds. She had trapped them on their own world and stripped them of any mental capacity to enable them to evolve again into a race that could cause any trouble. He hated her for that.

In fact, he hated The Four more than could be imagined. When his world was first visited and nurtured, he had been one of the few who had ascended, as he liked to think of it, to being one of those that nurtured and managed all of creation, sitting just below The Four in power.

Even during that time, and as he helped to nurture worlds, he had become aware that there was more to be done than just set races on the path to peace and love. He had understood that this needed to be balanced with greed and hate—only then would races evolve into their full potential. No one else had seen this need, and so he had to try and balance the essence himself without the knowledge of the others. As time progressed he had become more and more confident in his abilities, and was sure he was right.

Elgred had stopped him then, and had taken away some of the knowledge that he had been given. Framin had been tasked with nurturing small, insignificant planets, where no sentient beings were ever going to grow.

How he hated them, he seethed. He had managed though, even on these small worlds, to create destruction and fear, and had fed off it. Over time he had gained back some of what he once knew, and he used this to hide himself away, plotting the day he would rise up to challenge The Four. With the onset of

170

this world and his ability to start to influence them early, he now felt he was getting closer to his desire. He was not going to be undone this time.

Elgred's reluctance to directly interfere with a race's evolution would be his undoing. Framin had no such compunction; he would succeed for sure, and when he did the whole of the universe would embrace the darkness, and he would be the god he was born to be.

It was time to connect and see if he could advance his plans and set this race on the road to self-destruction and hate. He would nurture them to a future full of fear and death and darkness. He would create a race like no other that had a thirst for conquest, and conquest in the name of evil.

He made his way down to the rooms that were under his palace. He had one that he liked more than the others. He didn't need a specific place to connect, but he had manufactured himself a portal like the ones he had given to the Gouarong, and he did find it useful. Of course, such a thing was just a fabrication of the essence—once you knew how to treat it and manipulate it, a portal was not needed. These beings, though, did not have his knowledge, and because of that it was easier to connect with them this way. He could control them through the portals and influence them to do his bidding. He loved the feeling of despair he got when he connected with the lines—it made him sure that he was heading in the right direction.

He stood before the portal, and before he immersed himself in the lines he looked around his room. It was amazing how much living on this planet and being present in human form gave him so much pleasure. Once he managed to corrupt all the lines, he thought, he might stay here, make himself the leader of the whole planet, and just enjoy the gradual demise of this race and immerse himself in the debauchery of the whole thing. Such thoughts filled him with desire.

He reached out his hands and his thoughts, and delved into the lines.

He could feel his Gouarong, he could feel the despair infiltrating the lines of essence, he could feel the fear begin to grow and dissipate among the populations of the cities that his Gouarong ruled. He started to push his thoughts out to each of the cities.

Something was wrong. He realized that they weren't all there. He could tell that Santarish and Kahilja were not connected. It was strange, but then he often had trouble with one or more of his Gouarong. Giving them power sometimes made them more ambitious than he would like. He decided to check on the others first and then come back to these two, and visit them in person if necessary. He needed to be sure that they understood they needed to do what he wanted without question.

He let his thoughts reach out to the others, and what he saw pleased him immensely. Each of them had completed the portal and had started to enslave the local population. They were feeding the lines with fear, and this was rippling out to the local populace and creating more unrest and greed. In fact, there was more fear and disruption than he'd anticipated at each of the cities—that could only be a good thing. He was pleased, very pleased his plans were coming together. He would feed the fear and hate, and he and his Gouarong would infect this race with what they wanted. But he knew it would not be quick. He could wait, though. Time had no real meaning to him, and he was creating what he wanted.

CHAPTER 22
TIME TO START

Elji and Talisha came back to the gathering, and it was as if no one had even noticed them leaving—they were still eating and enjoying each other's company. As they walked in Dregar looked up and smiled. He turned to Amaran and whispered to him in order to get his attention. Amaran leaned in, then looked up. A smile also appeared on his face. Elji and Talisha walked over to them.

"I see that Talisha has been looking after you?" said Dregar. "You seem to be more than you were when you left." He laughed, then stood and took Elji first by the hand, and then embraced him. "I wasn't sure what might happen, but I see you chose a path that brought you back to us."

"Yes," said Elji. "Did you know of this and what might be?"

"No," said Dregar. "But I long ago ceased to be amazed at what can happen. I did know that coming here would lead you to a choice. I didn't know what those choices might be, and indeed I still don't, but judging by your current appearance, I guess that you have made a decision that has set you on a path that will help us all in the end. These people, as I told you before, have no malice in them, and their only need is to embrace the good and help it to flourish. That is why they nurture and are able to utilize the power that creates the galrass. The universe would not allow it any other way."

Shamshar spoke then. "I see that something has grown between you and my daughter—there is a change in her also. I can feel it. She has become part of something greater than herself, and for that I am grateful. Each of us, if we are lucky enough, gets to embrace something that has come from the purity of the essence. It seems to me that she has found that something."

"Thank you, Father," said Talisha. "I was not expecting this either, but as you say, we are bound by what we are, and what we are is not always what we expect." She smiled at him and they also embraced. "You know I have to go with him?"

"Yes," Shamshar said. "I know that this will now be your path, and I can only rejoice that you have found such a connection. It is, as you know, not always our fate to reach such a state, though we all hope that someday it will come. I guess it calls for some kind of celebration? Dregar, do we have time? I would like at least to acknowledge that my daughter has found what she is, and for us all to share in that finding."

"Shamshar," said Dregar. "You know as well as I do that such things will be what they will be. The fact that this has occurred means that we have the time. And in any case, we can manage that process, can't we?"

Shamshar stood. "My people, hear me." Silence fell across all the people that were gathered, and indeed across the whole community. "My daughter Talisha, has found one that begins to make her whole with the universe. She has discovered that thing which few of us are lucky enough to experience. She has become whole with the essence by combining herself with another. She must leave us now and go on her journey to accomplish all that she can, but before she does we will embrace them with everything we have."

He stopped talking and bowed his head. As he did he started to let out a note so low that Elji felt it would rumble through the ground. Others joined in with the tonal chant, and it built to a sound so magical it flowed through every being. Just as Elji thought it could go no further, the alhitan joined in, adding a further layer of harmony that seemed impossible. With their joining, the luminescence all around them began to rise and turn in toward each other and spiral into a cone, and kept going till it was above both Elji and Talisha. It continued to rise and rise—it was magical. A crescendo of sound and sight was reached, and then the tonal chant ceased and the luminescence descended onto Elji and Talisha in a slow shower of pure rapture.

They both stood and allowed themselves to be enveloped by the moment. People walked towards them, and each one touched them as if to gather a part of the magic for themselves.

Finally Dregar approached. "Now we are ready," he said. "Let's go and do what we must do."

"Yes," said Elji. "I know that now I know more than I did, but it just raises more questions in my mind as to what we must do and how best to unravel what is already done.

"One thing you could settle for me though. I asked you about your stick, if you remember, and I know that it, amongst what we are about to do, is nothing. But I would like to know why you brandish your stick."

Dregar laughed. "It's very simple, really. When you have

175

a lot to think about and you need to do something, it is always more difficult to focus the mind on what is needed. Over the years I have developed a pattern with my stick for things I need to do. I brandish it, and it makes me think about what I need to do. It is nothing more than a reminder." He smiled at Elji.

"I thought it might be something like that. While I was learning, a thought crossed my mind about using symbolism to create certain states. I think we may be able to teach many people how to manipulate the essence this way. It is something to think about once we have dealt with the current situation. Anyway, I am ready when you are. Let's go and see how we can help." He turned to Talisha. "Are you ready?"

"Yes," she replied. "I am — I go where you go."

The three of them looked at each other and Dregar spun his stick, laughing as he did so.

They arrived in the small building where the others were gathered. Dregar struck out his stick as Bethrod tried to impale them on his sword. The sword flew from his hand.

"Well, that's a nice welcome," said Dregar.

"Sorry," said Bethrod. "I thought we had something in place that stopped others from just butting in." He looked around at the others.

"It's OK," said Elji. "You did have. But I pushed us through anyway." He smiled.

Saloora and Bremen looked at him. "Elji?" they both said with surprise in their voices.

"Yes," he said. "It's a bit of a story. When we are done with all this we can tell it over a drink."

"What is the situation now?" asked Dregar.

"We have control of two of the portals, and have managed to turn the lines back in on themselves. We now have all the

Jalaria waiting for the word to take over the rest. As far as we know Framin is still here, and we were waiting for you. Now that you are here, if we are all agreed I can give the word and we can make the final push," said Bethrod.

"OK," said Elji. "But before we do I think it's best if we can get ourselves closer to where we think Framin is. We will have to be there to confront him as your Drendrak and Jalaria attack. If he feels something happening he may well go to help."

"I agree," said Cloin. "I would prefer to be in a position to see the whites of his eyes before we make any decision on the final assault."

"We may find that along the way to find Framin in his palace, we'll come across unexpected distractions," said Dregar. "If that's the case, it is imperative that Elji and I get to Framin. You should all try and engage whatever it is that gets in our way, and then come and help as soon as possible. Are we agreed?"

Everyone nodded.

"That's it then—let's go," said Bethrod.

They made their way from their hiding place and across a short open space to the edge of the buildings, and began to move towards the palace. As they reached the palace Naimer said, "Does it seem strange that we haven't seen anything living as yet?"

"It may be nothing," said Bethrod. "Framin is supremely confident in his ability to defend himself, and though I have never been here before, I hear that it is the palace itself that we should fear. So let's be cautious from now on."

They entered and moved down a short corridor into a room, where they all stopped dead in their tracks. The room was the most beautiful any of them had ever seen. To each of them it was different, but to each it was perfect.

Elji spoke. "Let me deal with this." He stood in the middle of the room and closed his eyes. Within seconds the décor of the room started to unravel, and in its place was a plain, square bare-walled room. "Framin was using the essence to make the room appear to each of us as the most perfect it could be. A very clever ruse indeed. I'm sure that we will face more of this."

As he finished speaking a deafening noise filled the room, and something of unimaginable proportions lumbered in. They scattered, and the beast lurched for them.

It had a huge head, much like a large bull, with horns that must have been four feet long. Its arms were three times longer than they needed to be, and its hands were tipped with claws that were each as big as a normal human. Its torso looked like that of a bloated alligator and was ridged with spikes. It stood in the middle of the room and bellowed again.

"It's a grehonaught," shouted Elji. "I have seen such in my dreams as a boy. Don't let it touch you, as it will induce exquisite pleasure, but at the same time it will suck the life force from you."

Cloin shouted. "You all go. Naimer and I will take care of this." They turned to face the beast. The others ran toward a door at the rear of the room and passed through.

***

Cloin and Naimer separated and stood on each side of the grehonaught, which was looking at them. Then it charged. Naimer jumped and spun out of its reach, and as she did so she sent a line of essence into the being, raking it across its back. It shook itself and looked at her again. She threw another line of essence. It shook again.

"Well, that doesn't seem as if it will work," she said.

The grehonaught lurched for her again, and as it did Cloin cleaved at its long arm with his sword. His sword smoked and the grehonaught pulled back.

"OK," he said. "It doesn't seem to like steel. We are going to have to do this the old fashioned way." He leapt at it, brandishing his sword. Naimer unleashed her own sword and came at it from a different angle.

Cloin and Naimer danced round the thing, inflicting injury where they could. The grehonaught was whirling and screaming in rage, but they were too quick for it, and after a short while it was tiring. They closed in. As they did so the grehonaught shot out its long arm and got hold of Naimer. She screamed in pain, then went limp in its big claw.

Cloin threw himself at the beast and began to hack away with all his might. It lurched and flailed, and as it did so it threw Naimer against the wall and she fell lifeless to the floor.

Cloin had never been so focused on anything, and he set about slicing his way through the thing. He jumped and twirled and attacked every angle, but he was tiring and it was difficult to tell if he was winning at all. His sword was starting to slip in his hand as he sweated and grunted at the effort.

He jumped forward towards the head, and as he did he slid to his back and along the floor under the beast. As he went he brought up his sword and carved a long deep gash into the stomach of the grehonaught, much as he had done with the eaglion. It began to collapse, and he was sure it was going to fall on him. With his last bit of strength he rolled away just as the grehonaught crashed to the floor. He lay on his back, sucking in air till he was able to move, and then crawled his way towards his sister.

He reached out his hand and tilted her face toward him.

She was grey in color, as if death had already taken hold of her, but he thought he had felt a movement. He pulled himself toward her and cradled her head in his lap. He could feel her breathing — yes, he was certain he could — but it was very shallow.

He took hold of her graithe and closed his eyes, and sent out a thought. *Tragarg, Naimer needs you.*

He appeared beside them, looked at the situation, and took hold of Naimer. "You will have to take care of yourself," he said to Cloin as he disappeared with Naimer.

"Yes, OK," said Cloin to empty space. He lay again on the floor, and thought he might just take a few more minutes to regain his strength.

***

Bethrod, Dregar, Elji, Talisha, Saloora, and Bremen were making their way down the corridor that led from the door at the back of the room. They could hear the noise coming from what they had left behind, but it was muffled, and the further they went the less it could be heard.

It appeared that the corridor they were in was taking them down and to the left on a very slight gradient. It wasn't very long, but was getting darker as they went. Dregar held out his hand, and a luminescent glow appeared from the length of his stick, just enough to make a difference for them.

The corridor came to an intersection that led both left and right. They needed to make a decision.

"Elji, you take Talisha and Bremen and go left," Dregar said. "We will go right."

Bremen set off to the left and Elji and Talisha followed. Without the light from Dregar it was dark, but not so dark that they couldn't see at all. In only a few short strides they came to a door and pushed through. In the center of the room was a tiny black stone, floating above the floor at about head height, hovering in silence.

Bremen spoke. "What do you think this is?"

"It looks like some kind of galrass," Talisha said, and took a step toward it. "Though it doesn't appear to be solid, and doesn't have any indication of the universe in it. We know where every galrass that we have created is, and this is not one of them. Perhaps if I can take a while, I might be able to study it and see what I think it is." She looked round at them both.

"Don't go any closer, Talisha," said Elji. "There is something odd in the feel of this room, and it will most certainly have something to do with this object."

"It's OK," she said, and took a step closer. "It's tiny; what harm can come?"

As she took her step closer Bremen noticed that she diminished in size. Indeed, as he looked around he realized that the whole room was bigger than when they had first entered, and the stone itself was a little larger.

"Elji, Talisha, we need to get out!" said Bremen. "Quickly — something is happening!" He turned and made for the door. As he turned he noticed that Elji and Talisha now looked a very long way off, and indeed were moving further away as he looked.

Elji and Talisha looked at Bremen and could tell that they were in some kind of a gravitational pull that was dragging them towards the stone, but in a non-dimensional sense. The stone was getting bigger, the room now looked huge, and Bremen was only just visible in the distance.

Elji sent him a message. *It's OK, Bremen. Talisha and I will see this thing through, you go and help the others.*

Bremen got the message and left the room, pulling the door closed behind him.

Elji looked back towards the stone, and he could see that it had grown even more and they were being pulled toward it. "Do you want to see where this leads?" he asked Talisha. "I am certain I could put us back outside the room, but whatever this is might be important."

"Yes," said Talisha. "It's here for a reason, and it must have something to do with Framin, so let's see what happens."

They looked back at the stone and could see that they were now speeding toward it, and as they got closer it became more spherical and darker, and indeed bigger. It loomed larger and larger in their vision till all they could see was that they were heading straight into darkness. It was an eerie process, and it reminded Elji somewhat of his being pulled into the timeline, though he couldn't feel any malice in the darkness this time.

Faster and faster they travelled, all the time the darkness becoming more and more intense. They shot through what could only be described as an opening that sped toward them, and they were deposited into a pool. There was no water in the pool, but there was a huge cascade of universal essence coming from nowhere and into the pool.

The pool swam and moved with life. As they looked they could see a myriad of different life forms ebbing and flowing in the pool, some huge like the grehonaught and some tiny like flies. None of them noticed each other, and they didn't notice either Elji or Talisha.

As they looked around the edge of the pool came into focus, and sitting there as if on nothing, but dangling their legs, were Ichancha and Charina.

Charina was waving at them and beckoning them over.

"My, my Elji," said Charina. "How you have changed. This must be Talisha?"

CHAPTER 23
FRAMIN'S UNDOING.

Bremen caught up with the others, who were standing at the entrance to another door and had not entered the room beyond.

Dregar looked at him and said, "Elji and Talisha?"

"We found something strange, and they have gone to investigate," he replied. "It seems I was not needed, so I came to see what help I could give here."

"Are they OK?" asked Dregar.

"I think so," said Bremen. "They were heading toward some kind of confluence within the universe. I am not sure where they actually are or what danger they are in. I think that Elji will cope with whatever it is they face."

"OK, let's see what is behind this door," said Bethrod.

The room was empty. There were no other entrances or exits. They looked at each other.

"I am sure that Framin came this way," said Dregar. "There must be something we are not seeing."

"I can find him," said Bethrod. "Just give me a minute. I

always have an essence line following him so I can see what he is up to. He doesn't know it's there, and I keep it some distance from him." He closed his eyes. His eyes snapped back open. "Strange. The trace seems to come into this room, and then it's like it is disconnected. That can't happen. The trace can follow him anywhere in the universe. So unless he has discovered it, in reality it means he is not in this universe, and I just don't know what that means. How can something not be of this universe?"

Dregar grunted. "Well, I suppose that if we accept that all things are possible, then something not being of this universe must also be possible. Though in all my time I have never experienced or even contemplated such an occurrence. If that is really the case, then that means everything we think we know is in question. I can't imagine that to be the case. Elgred and Charina have never even suggested that there is more to everything than the original four. Though I suppose from a conceptual perspective we could imagine that they must have come from somewhere themselves. We have discussed this, but decided that some things must just be what they are.

"If we accept that something or someone created The Four… no, it's a concept too hard to comprehend. It would put us in a loop, because then we would be at the stage of wondering who created the creators of The Four. My best guess is that this black hole that Elgred and Charina know of has some influence on this, and has some ability to be able to hide essence lines. I am not sure; it's all very confusing, but it is interesting and amazing at the same time. I suggest we do two things. First, we give the order for the Drendrak to finish their takeover of the portals, and then we go back and see where Elji and Talisha are. I have a suspicion that where they have gone may lead us to a reckoning on all of this."

"I will send the call to the Drendrak," said Bethrod.

The others turned to leave the room and a sound erupted over them. It was a high pitched keening sound, which magnified in its intensity to a point where everything they were looking at was resonating with the sound, as if it were becoming insubstantial, as if it were melting away. There was an enormous whooshing sound, and suddenly Framin was standing in front of them. As he appeared they could see that he was attached to something behind him, a darkness that could not be explained and was not visible, but just as if it were a thought.

Bethrod and Saloora reacted and attacked straight away, drawing their swords and engaging Framin. Dregar and Bremen dropped their consciousness into the level of the essence and started their own attack on Framin from that level. As they did the room erupted and they could see a huge portal. A thick black line came into focus as it fed the portal, and then fed the other portals from this central one.

Everything expanded again, and they were now faced with the view of every portal that Framin had created via his Gouarong. They could see the Drendrak standing at each portal, fighting and struggling with the essence lines that were fed to and from the portals. Each of the portals was being fed from the one that Framin was standing over, and that was fed by the blackness beyond.

Framin raged at Saloora and Bethrod and swatted them aside. He turned to face Dregar and Bremen and smiled. "Ahh," he said. "I see we meet the manmade God and Elgred's messenger."

He clapped his hands together and started to emit a note. Dregar and Bremen were brought to their knees by the sound, and they felt like the essence was being pulled from them and fed into the blackness beyond Framin's portal. Dregar swirled his stick, and he and Bremen dissipated into the essence and swirled round Framin.

Framin could hear Dregar laughing. "Do you think that you were the only one that was taught by Elgred?" asked Dregar. "Do you think that only you understand how to manipulate the universal essence?"

They both reappeared on different sides of Framin, and though he was still emitting the tone they had shielded themselves from its disruptive force. Bethrod and Saloora had regained their feet, and were rushing back to oppose Framin again. Dregar swirled his stick again and a light engulfed Framin, which intensified when Bremen chanted a word or two. Saloora and Bethrod had reached him, and both struck out with force and speed, slicing through his skin.

Framin threw back his head and roared, and burst from his skin. In his place was a different form. No longer was he huge and bronzed, but was now small and slight, with a large head and eyes that blazed in their blackness. He looked to be made of black marble. What passed for his skin was alive with energy, and fizzled with sparks so much blacker than his skin that they seemed to shine.

He opened his mouth again and began to utter another sound. Just as he did so the portal next to him began to collapse. The Drendrak had wrestled the others free, and it was having an effect.

Saloora and Bethrod surged at him again, this time joined by Cloin. They all sliced at him in unison. Dregar and Bremen redoubled their attack. Framin recoiled in shock.

From the portal a thick black line emerged and engulfed Framin. He disappeared, and as he did a rush of fear escaped the portal, knocking them all backwards as it passed through them. Bremen and Dregar were rendered nearly senseless. Bethrod, Saloora, and Cloin collapsed and lay inert on the floor. The portal collapsed, and everything fell silent.

CHAPTER 24
QUANTANIUMS

"Charina!" said Elji. "Yes, this is Talisha. And you are right, I have changed." He smiled at her.

"Elgred and I wondered which path you would take, and I see you chose the one of life and enlightenment. I am pleased that is the way you went."

"It wasn't too difficult a choice," he said. "Though I have to admit, the thought of being unburdened of everything I know and everything that may happen to me did hold a lot of promise. I guess it must just be in my nature to be inquisitive," he laughed.

"Yes, perhaps," she said. "Though I think there is probably something more basic than that at work."

"Where are we?" asked Talisha. "And what is this thing we sit in or on?"

"That is a really good question—well, two really good questions," said Charina. "I am not sure I can explain it. When Ichancha fled, I just followed her, and we ended up here. I have been trying since to find out where we are and what this is, but the normal rules of the universe and the essence don't seem to apply here. It's an interesting phenomenon, though it does bring up some basic questions about everything we know. Ichancha doesn't know anything about this place, and since we came she has reverted to the intelligence of a small child and I can't get any sense from her. It's as if whatever she learned since she left us has left her again.

"As to what this is, I have some inclination that it is some kind of mirror into all the types of life in the universe. Though nothing I do to it seems to make the slightest bit of difference, and as you saw for yourselves interacting with it also has no impact on it. It's as if it has no substance, but is all substance at the same time. The only thing I have noticed is that where we seem to sit now there is a slight edge to the thing, though I can't see anything.

"While we have been here, every now and then there is a massive shift in this pool, and a planet seems to appear at the surface and then get engulfed. I wish I could speak to Elgred, but I find that I can't reach him, or anything else for that matter. So having you here, while it is nice to see you, it means that you are trapped here too."

Talisha dipped her hand into the substance again, and her face took on a quizzical look. "When we create the galrass and imbue it with the universe, we use a kind of pool that allows us to imprint the stone with the universe. It seems to me that this is a little like that thing, but different. It's as if we are on the other side of that pool. Looking at it from the outside in, if you see what I mean."

Elji looked at her and then at Charina. "What if what she says is right? What if somehow we are seeing everything, but from the reverse side? That would mean that no universal rules

190

would apply here—in fact, they would be the opposite of what we know."

"It's possible," said Charina. "Though I don't know how we could even test such a hypothesis. If nothing that we know works, then we can have no impact."

"Let me try something," said Talisha. She closed her eyes, dipped in her hands, and started a low tonal sound. The pool stirred and a white stone, interlaced with black lines and black specs, appeared on the surface. She opened her eyes.

They all looked at each other and then at the stone.

"It's a galrass," gasped Talisha. "But it's the opposite of what we usually create. What I did was chant the tonal opposite of what I would use to gather the universe together to inhabit a galrass back at home. I am not sure how it helps us, but perhaps we can use it."

"Wait," said Charina. "If we do this, and your theory of all this being the opposite of what we know, where would we be?"

"Also," said Elji, "why are we here? I know this may be difficult for you to accept, Charina, but if we are here beyond anything you ever knew existed, then it must be for some reason. Is there something we are supposed to see? To notice? The fact that we are here means that either someone has a complete understanding of the universal essence and wants us to know something, or everything we know is just not everything."

"OK," said Talisha. "Now I don't know, and can't comprehend the complexity of the problem you are suggesting. But I have a thought. If we suspect that, were we to use the galrass, we would find the exact opposite of what we know, then what if we could get to this exact position but from the other side? Would the rules that we know come back into play? Do you see what I mean? If we could get back here from the other side, then we must be able to influence it. What do you think?"

"What I think is this," said Charina, and she stood. Elji and Talisha were thrown into a whirlpool of black. Charina and Ichancha had gone. They found that they were hurtling toward the stone again.

"This is strange," said Elji. "I think that something is trying to keep us occupied while things unfold."

Their journey ended abruptly. This time they were in a huge room, colossal by any standards, and filled with essence lines of all kinds, most of them as black as anything they had seen. In front of them was a dias holding an orb, the same color, and standing next to it were two forms. One was a being as black as the orb itself, and the other was the double of Elgred.

"I thought that using this form might make you feel a little less disoriented," the Elgred double said. "I am Lhapso. I take it you have heard of me?" He smiled at them. "And this is Framin. Someone I have used for millennia—such an obedient tool."

"Lhapso?" said Elji. "But Elgred said you were gone, and that neither he nor Charina knew what had happened to you."

"True," said Lhapso. "But then, when you are trying to influence a universe and create something that suits you, you don't want anyone else interfering with your plans, do you? It was my hope that you would find a solution to your problem, and in doing so be eternally caught in a loop between the two quantaniums. What I hadn't counted on was that somehow you would stumble across a tool that would allow you to get back to where you wanted to be. That was very clever, Talisha. It is also interesting that some things seem to work in the quantanium. I hadn't counted on that."

"Quantaniums?" asked Elji. "What is a quantanium?"

Lhapso looked at them and decided something. "Seeing as you are going to be here forever unless I let you go, I might as well share what I am doing. As you know, I was one of the original four, and between us we created magnificent life forces, races, and planets. We were the masters of everything. But as with all things that are possible, I became restless in having to share my creations with others. I wanted to be The One, not one of The Four. I did speak to Elgred, Charina, and Ichancha about these things, and discussed with them the possibility of creating separate universes that adhered only to the rules of each one of us. They were not open to that discussion, and wanted all things to be shared. Their arguments were convincing; working together we could create much more, they said. We could balance each other out in our fervor to create, ensure we were seeding each race with the ability to evolve, and utilize the true beauty of the essence—on and on they went.

"What they failed to realize was that, actually, without the opposite of hope and love, then hope and love itself means nothing. There is nothing to measure it against. With darkness, there must be light, and so with love, there must be hate. We created and planned and evolved, and in doing that I discovered a dead star, something we had not noticed before, something we had ignored. I studied it, and realized that once through one of these dead stars there was a different quantum...think of it like a dimension. But being just a dimension means it is encapsulated by everything we know. A quantanium is beyond everything we know—it is the antithesis of everything we know, a new reality. It is not a dimension as you know it. It is beyond the essence—it is antiessence. I decided that this was my chance, a way I could create my own universe.

"The problem was that nothing was created there—it was

only in the destruction of things here in this universe that creation could happen there. So I had a choice; I stay and create with the others and be content with that, or I tip the balance and make sure of destruction, and so enable myself to accelerate the ability to create in the quantanium. It is why I engaged Framin. It is why I strive to ensure that darkness and destruction prevail enough for me to build my own reality. All of existence is frail and futile and fickle. I only need to influence its path towards self-destruction. Some is harder than others. Here on this planet there is a desire to destroy, and its path has been easier to influence than most in a very long time. I was going to leave you two where you were, stuck, but the fact that Talisha was able to create the galrass, but the opposite to the galrasses that are used in this dimension, meant that I can now accelerate the plan even further by utilizing the abilities she has uncovered. This means I can indulge in creation in the new quantanium. So to do that I am going to have to have Framin here absorb her essence and garnish her abilities." He smiled at them. "So I will leave you with each other now, and go and usher in more destruction."

He disappeared.

Framin turned then to face them. "Let's get this over with so I can return and finish off your co-conspirators."

***

Dregar and Bremen went to the others to make sure they were OK. Saloora, Cloin, and Bethrod were senseless, and it was as if there was no life left in them at all, though Cloin and Bethrod were definitely breathing. Dregar closed his eyes and called to Tragarg, and he appeared, took one look at Bethrod and Cloin, and clutched on to each of them. Then he was gone.

Bremen sat on the floor next to Saloora, and Dregar sat

down next to him. They both looked at her, and Dregar dropped his head. "I think he said that we have lost her. I don't feel her essence here at all."

Bremen lifted her head and cradled it; he too could feel that she was lifeless. He closed his eyes and sent out his thoughts into the universe. He could feel her essence then; it was beginning to amalgamate itself to the whole. His pain was immense — he had only known her a short while, but it had been the deepest real feeling he had ever had. He began to panic.

"Dregar, I need her here! I can't lose that which I have only just found. What can we do?"

"Bremen, she will always be with you. You preach and know the true beauty of the essence, and you know she is never truly gone. You will find her again in all things you cherish. She is a part of you, and you a part of her. It is a transient pain, and one you know not to be real."

Bremen looked at him — it felt so real, that was the problem, and it felt like loss and it felt like pain. He turned his head to the ceiling and cried as he had never cried before, and as he did his pain and his grief changed into an empty space, an emptiness he felt deep in his heart. He realized something at that point. This was the difference in being human; this was why good and bad influenced people, because no matter how strong your core belief, losing something you loved was pain, and pain was raw and real.

He had a thought — he could let himself go now and join her. Then the pain would go. Yes, that was what he would do. As that thought materialized he heard her — he heard her speak.

"Bremen, you are the people. You are their salvation and truth, and you are needed there. I will always be part of you, and my love will help you create a greater understanding of those who strive to be the best they are. We will meet again in another place and time. I will never leave you. You and I are bound for all time; my essence is your essence. I am you and you are me. I am Ahhbreshemen, the source of your essence to do good on this world. I am your voice in the essence—I am your message of hope, and I will spread this hope for you. It is what I was destined to be."

He wept. He wept because he knew she was right, and he wept because such things must need be.

***

Bethrod woke. He was back in his palace, and beside his bed was Tragarg. "Cloin and Naimer?" he asked. "Where are they? Are they OK?"

Tragarg spoke. "Both are alive, barely, though I think we can pull them through.

You fared better than them."

"How long have I been here?"

"Only an hour or so. Do you remember anything?" Tragarg asked.

"Yes," he said. "I remember confronting Framin with the others. We attacked him, and then something so black came from his portal." He frowned. "I have not seen anything of its like before. The desolation that was emitted was so intense it sucked everything away from me."

"Dregar called me, and when I got there you were senseless," said Tragarg. "I had already been and brought Cloin back. He has not regained consciousness, so I don't know what happened to him yet. Naimer is the same, but as I said we have them in time and we can heal them. Though what darkness they have seen and how they will be affected I don't know."

"What of the battles in the city?" asked Bethrod. "How do

they go?"

"The Drendrak and their lords have won through in every city. All the portals are destroyed, and now they are pushing through to take control and deal with the dregs of any resistance. All the Drendrak are immersed in holding the portals, and cleansing them of fear and hate. Two have fallen from the effort, but they secured the portals nonetheless. There is a massive task to undertake now in consolidating the power we have grasped, and in controlling lands at such distances. It will be an undertaking that will take years, if not decades, to accomplish. We must set these people on the right path, and bring a chance for a greater future."

"OK," said Bethrod. "I think that now my help is best suited here. Dregar, Bremen, and the others will have to complete what they do without my help. Come, my friend. Let us tend to our families, and then let us go about holding together an empire and building a future worthy of our efforts."

***

Framin began to move towards Elji and Talisha. His gait was nonchalant—he was in no rush.

Elji close his eyes and pulled on a connection in the essence and threw it at Framin. His skin cracked again, but this time in place of the black ebony image there stood a whirling mass of black lines, swirling and speeding round each other, holding together in a human like form. It continued to push outwards and then retracted. The thing kept moving. As it did, it started to solidify into a much more recognizable human form. This time it was the image of Elji's mother.

"Elji," it said. "It's so good to see you again. We have missed you so much." She reached out a hand to him.

Elji looked at the hand and recoiled. His eyes shot up, and

197

now Talisha stood in front of him.

"It's OK," she said. "It's not real, it's just an illusion." She reached out further for him and touched his shoulder.

Elji reacted and moved himself through space and behind Framin. He pushed out a line of essence and it began to coil round Framin. It was so white and pure it was brilliant and blinding. He cast out more and more till it encompassed Framin.

Framin stood stock still. He shuddered, and all the light that Elji had cast began to grey and get darker and darker, and was reaching back toward Elji. Elji let the line go and it fell.

Framin turned and looked at him and laughed. "Do you think that a mere mortal can possibly have the power to do harm to me? I have had millennia of understanding how to manipulate the universe and how to turn it to my needs." He laughed and began to chant.

"Talisha," Elji called. "We have to go now. He intends to turn us into raw essence — we will be lost."

"Where can we go?" she screamed.

"Into the portal," said Elji. "I have a plan."

He took her hand and catapulted them in. They were back hurtling toward the black hole.

"Do you still have the galrass you created just now?" he asked.

"I do," she said. "It's still in my hand."

"OK, good. I think we have one chance to finish this once and for all. I need to go and get Framin to come and follow us, and we need to get into the quantanium that Lhapso spoke of. Once there I think we can use your galrass and mine to close the link between the two realities once and for all. If we can do that, then we will trap both Framin and Lhapso. Though I doubt it will be forever.

"We need to swap galrasses; you'll have mine, and I will need the one you just created. When we get to the edge of the black hole I am going to steady us between the two realities, and when I do I need you to unleash the whole of the universe from my galrass. I need you to set it free. I will make sure you are expelled into the current reality. I am hoping that the sheer magnitude of everything will collapse the connection, and in doing this it will fill the void of this black hole and every other there is, and will block them off. It will create a partition between the two universes, where both exist on separate sides but are blocked by the mass of the entirety of everything.

"I am not entirely sure what may be created from this as the two types of essence mix, but we can figure that out once we have corrected the problem, and we can get Elgred to solve it. I will push through, then will use your galrass to return to this side if I can. If I can get back to where Lhapso had us trapped, I can get free from there, knowing what we now know. Here, take my galrass."

They swapped the stones with each other.

"OK," said Elji. "I am going to see where Framin is and get him to follow us."

Talisha hoped he would come back soon—she could see that she was rushing toward oblivion.

***

Elji reappeared in the room. Framin was still there with his arms immersed in the lines emanating from the portal. Elji attacked him, encasing him again with the lines of essence. Framin again shrugged them off, but this time he rushed for Elji.

Elji pushed himself back into the portal with his thoughts and Framin followed him. They hurtled toward the black hole, and Framin attacked Elji with a lattice of black lines that tried to tighten themselves around him. Elji shifted himself in space and the lines closed in on themselves. He could see that Talisha was very close to the convergence of the two reality types. He willed himself to her and caught her hand just as they reached the joining. He spun them out of the vortex and watched Framin turn and try and stay with them, but he was almost through.

"Now," shouted Elji.

Talisha took his galrass and spun it in her hand, undoing the binding that held the universe in the stone. Elji pushed himself through and everything erupted.

***

The whole of time and everything that was real and unreal paused. A great blast of light and dark collided. Talisha was thrown from her current position and fell to the ground inside the room in Framin's palace.

There was no sign of either Elji or Framin.

The portal in the center of the room was lifeless save for a kind of shimmering glass that was alive with lines and specks. It looked like the surface of a lake lit by moonlight that had been disturbed by a stone dropped in it.

She reached out a hand and tried to feel what was there, but as her hand approached it, it moved away from her touch. No matter where she tried to reach there was nothing there.

CHAPTER 25
PAST, PRESENT, AND FUTURE

Elji and Framin were suspended in what could only be described as a void. It had no substance to it of any kind. Neither of them could feel any kind of essence, or any form of life force. Elji had suspected that they would be catapulted into this quantanium that Lhapso had mentioned, and he was confused as to how they could be where they were. He remembered then something that Dregar had said to him.

"All things are not only possible, but in all probability exist in some form somewhere in the universe."

That gave him hope. If that were the case, he should be able to get from here to where he wanted to go. He opened his hand, and though he couldn't see it he knew that he still held the galrass that Talisha had created.

He began to think and run his finger along the lines in the galrass. The reality around him changed, and he found himself standing on a green mound where a pyramid shaped majestic temple towered over him, the likes of which he had never seen or even imagined. Huge stones of every color possible glistened from the sides of the temple. It was impossible to describe, save that they were colorescent, a word he made up for the image.

Vast though the structure was, he could see that near the top was an opening with some form of light emitting from it. He tried to will himself to the opening but nothing happened. He tried again. Again nothing. He sat down and began to run over what had just happened in his mind to see if there was anything he could discover that may aid him.

He looked at the galrass again, and he could see that it was just a plain white stone—there were no lines or specks on it at all.

He looked up again. In front of him one of the stones in the pyramid changed its form and revealed an opening to the building. With no other plan in mind, he walked forward and entered the building.

He was in a corridor where every side was flat and seamless, and it sloped upwards and looked to switch back on itself. He walked for hours, switching back and forth and always going up. There was nothing to give him any perspective of how far he had come or how high he was, as the corridor rose and fell in an even gradient. It was disconcerting.

He came to a point to make the switch back again, and as he traversed up this portion there was an opening on his left, the first he had seen. He stopped and went in.

The room was adorned with artefacts. As he looked around he had no idea what any of them were. Artwork on the walls depicted human like beings, each wearing only a small loincloth. Many images showed them looking up at the sky, and in the background were great pyramids like the one he was in, but none of them of the same stone or the same stature.

Many of the men and women wore masks that looked like

buffalo or lions, or some kind of beetle. All of them were regal looking, some wielding spears, and all of them were drawn in profile, so he could get no real sense of how their faces looked. Antelope and other animals lay around as if from a hunt. Wheeled vehicles were pulled by horses. He saw images of stars in the sky, and of moons and suns.

As he went around the room the people seemed to change, and the buildings they were standing near changed too. The people became more like those he knew in his village and in the city. The buildings were much more familiar.

At one particular image he stopped and gasped. There in the painting was the palace of Bremen, and the people were people he knew from that place.

He looked around again, and realized that as he had been walking, he had been going upwards and around. It was an illusion that the room was just a room—it was never ending, going around and around and up.

He walked back down past the images he had seen.

He stopped and looked at the wall again. On it he could see images of people. This time they were much more primitive in nature, with wooden spears and clubs. Huge animals the likes of which he had never seen before roamed the land. Some had necks that were long with small heads and massive bodies. Others were smaller and much more fierce looking, with great jaws and teeth. He could see some type of birds in the sky. He had never seen their like before.

A thought began to coalesce in his mind. He looked up again and decided that he would go that way, as it was where he had seen the opening. Up he went, passing the artwork he had already seen and passing new images of people and places and buildings. As he walked there was a continual change in

203

the pictures.

He stopped again. He could still see people, but they wore different clothing and the buildings were of a different shape and size altogether, and they were packed together. There were many tall buildings sticking into the skyline, covered in what he assumed was glass, some taller than others but all crammed in together. He could see some kind of shiny, colored carts that had wheels but no horses to pull them. People were sitting in them.

He stopped again and looked round, realizing that while he had been walking, he had seen not a series of different images, but a continual one that changed and curved as he went. He realized that what he was seeing was the history of a people.

At that point his thoughts were confirmed. This was the history and the future of his people. This was the story of his planet.

He walked back down a bit to where he had seen the image of the palace he knew that Bremen lived in, and looked down and looked up. He went up again. As he went he noticed that some of the imagery he had seen as he had walked past was changing. The overall evolution felt and mainly looked the same, but the images were changing to depict different outcomes.

He went back down again and walked up again. Different again. He stopped at an image that held him mesmerized — an image of his planet from a great distance, from space as he knew it. As he walked the image took him closer to the planet, and he could see that it was desolated. There did not seem to be any life left on the planet at all.

Again he went back down, and again he started to go up. This time he came to the tall buildings. They had changed, and above them huge vehicles that looked like cities with wings were suspended in the sky. Up and up he went, and on and on the imagery went.

He stopped again, and this time he sat down and said, "All right, I get it."

A light appeared and hovered in front of him, growing in size. Elji stepped into it, and as he passed through he found he was standing on a ledge, and behind him was the door he had seen in the pyramid from the ground. He realized he was overlooking his world.

"Welcome, Elji," said a voice.

Elji turned, and behind him were Elgred, Charina, and Ichancha. He smiled at them. "Just when you think you begin to understand things, something comes along and shakes it all up for you, doesn't it?" Elji said.

Charina came over to him, a smile on her face. "Sometimes, Elji, things are not about what you understand, but about what you believe," she said. "I have someone else we think you should meet."

From a door further behind came another being that looked just like Elgred. "We meet again, Elji. I am Lhapso." He too smiled.

"I am confused," said Elji. "Completely confused. I thought that you had lost contact with Lhapso and Ichancha! I have just seen Lhapso with Framin, and we have just thrown a whole new universe into existence to block a black hole."

"Yes," said Lhapso. "Those things are all true, and this reality you see is now a future consequence of that action. I am sure you surmised by your journey up here that there are many future possibilities to your world, and each action taken in what you call the present shapes that future. We are all working to make sure that your race ascends to be the best that it can be.

205

What we have told you, what you have seen was true in that time and place, and that existence. But now you sit with us in a future possibility based on your current actions. We wanted you to see how your choices make a difference in what might be. The images you passed along your way are only the possible futures of your world, and you can help influence them."

"You have come a long way in a short time Elji," said Elgred. "We want you to know something—I want you to think of it like this. We are already looking at you from your distant future. We know what outcome we would like, and we are working with you to reach that outcome. If you and any you recruit to your cause—and there will be many along the way—fail in your tasks, so will the possible future reality for you. We are talking to you and watching you from what we want that to be. One truth we have told you in all this is that we can't directly interfere in what you as a race do to change your future. Only you can do that for yourselves. We can give you certain information and we can give you certain tools, but we cannot tell you what to do; that must be your choice. Each of the scenarios that you saw are future possibilities for you all, and amazing and marvelous things can come to be."

"The information you were given when you were on Talisha's world is real. You will see all those you love die, and you will live longer than anyone you know by thousands of years. You have been chosen for a task, which is to shepherd your world into the future on the path it needs to follow. You have to create a society—you will have to recruit people and show them the way. You will have to give them the understanding they need to be able to help you on your journey. You will see them come and go, but always you will be there ushering them through and keeping your race on track."

"Let me get this straight then," said Elji. "We are speaking from a possible future that hasn't happened yet; speaking to you in a further future that you hope will be by influencing what is happening now? I think that at this stage I am just going to have to accept what you say. Though given that much of what you have told me already has been only partial truths, how am I to know that what you tell me now is the truth?"

Ichancha came to him then and put her hand on his head. It spun; visions whirled through his mind and a truth unfolded.

Elji looked up at them and could not speak. When he did find his voice to speak, it was as if what Ichancha had shown him had enabled him to accept the visions and digest them.

"I have two questions," he said. "What is this place, and what of Framin?"

"Within the walls of this construct lies every possible future for every possible world," said Ichancha. "Depending on which world you enter from, the futures of that world will be shown in the corridor and rooms. If you have the knack you can see the futures of other worlds, but to do that you need incredible understanding. We use it to watch what happens. I suppose this is our home. It does not sit in any timeframe that anyone could know, or in any place in space. It just is. We did not create this thing. When we first gained what could be classed as consciousness it was here, and we have utilized it since. It is indeed a conundrum, as it existed outside of all things before anything was even brought into existence. We have discussed it at length, and we have no answer to what it is or how it is. It just is, and we have accepted that. Perhaps we can discuss it at length with you over time.

"As for Framin, you need now go back and take care of him to ensure that he doesn't influence your world in the current present. He and his influence will continue to be something you will have to deal with. There is no dark without light, and there is no love without hate. Both these things are truisms, as has been told to you before. Your task is to ensure that his side of all things does not outweigh yours. It will be your eternal battle, and you will be sorely tested at times in your future. Some battles you may win and some you may lose, but overall you must be the greater influence. Your world is now in the hands of you and your people. At this juncture in your time we have to leave you to build whatever you can. We have spent more time than we should to try and get through this phase, and we have come close to directly influencing things and breaking our own code.

"You will have to work with Bethrod, Bremen, Dregar, and Talisha. You will have to create a society within your society — a group of people that can influence others and bring about great change. You will have endless work to do, but first you must finish what is started, and then you must rebuild your world from the conquest that has been made by you all. Bremen and Dregar can help you bring the message to all. Bethrod and his children and his Drendrak can help you organize and run the nations. Talisha will be your light when things get dark again. She has the knowledge of the universe and its construction. Listen to her council. She will be your ear for all things.

"By the time you have finished with Framin you will have lost much, and there will be grieving to be done, but that must wait till that task is finished. Go now, and do what you must do. We will be absent in your near current future — we have other priorities. Dregar will always be able to reach us at need. When you expanded the universe from the galrass you cut off some of your connections with others in the universe, as you created paradoxes that are yet to resolve themselves. So some of those worlds you have seen may not now be open to you. You will need them, and if you find you do then I am sure you will find a way.

"Elji, we have great hope for your race, and we hope that at some point one of you will come to join us in guiding the rest of everything on its path."

They all came to him, and they embraced. Elji felt that he was losing much, and being given an awful lot of responsibility for one person. Still, if they thought he had the ability, who was he to argue? They had brought him a very long way in a very short time.

He looked up at them again and they faded.

CHAPTER 26
FRAMIN'S CAPTURE

Elji was back in the void and Framin was just in front of him. It was as if all that had happened had taken not even a fraction of a second. He grabbed Framin and fingered his galrass again.

They were both back in Framin's chamber, next to the portal, and Talisha was there alongside Dregar, who had made his way to the chamber. Elji threw his essence lines at Framin, and Dregar joined in by creating a lattice of energy around him. Framin raged and struggled; however, this time he was unable to shrug off the effects of the attack.

Elji took control of the lattice that Dregar had constructed and turned the lines into those of the antiessence, the same he had seen while dealing with Lhapso in the void.

Framin was helpless to change anything. Every time he tried something it just made the lattice stronger. He fumed and struggled. Inside the lattice he was changing from one kind of being to another. Nothing was working. When he touched the lattice he screamed, and a little more energy drained from him. He was trapped.

Dregar, Elji, and Talisha sat.

"What did you do?" asked Dregar. "I wasn't expecting it to be that easy to stop him."

"Something I learned while trying things at different points. I don't think I can sustain this forever—it is made based on something that doesn't exist here. I have created an illusion that is the opposite of everything that Framin knows. It will thwart him for quite some time, I am sure. It is powerful enough to last for years, but not forever.

"A lot has happened in a short time, and we need to speak about it. Right now, though, we must get Framin somewhere we can contain him. It's not in our nature to destroy him, so we must work with what we have. Hopefully someday we may be able to persuade him that our way is right and he has been wrong."

"That," said Dregar, "may take a very long time. He has been planning and scheming for millennia."

"I know," said Elji. "But still we must try."

"I suggest then," said Dregar, "that we return to Bremen's palace. We can deal with whatever is needed there."

"Yes," said Elji. "I agree. Once we have done that we must get everyone together and discuss what must be done going forward."

"Then let's go. There is no better time than the now." Dregar lifted his stick and twirled it in a pattern. They were suddenly back at Bremen's palace in a room that Elji had not seen before.

"Where are we?" he asked.

"We are below the palace in an area where the palace stores its goods. I thought it best to be out of the way. Even in this state I don't want Framin to be able to influence whoever he sees."

Talisha looked at them both and spoke. "I am tired. If he

is secured, can we not go and get some rest, and then see what must be done?"

"I am sorry, Talisha," said Elji. "Yes, you are right. Come on—I will get you settled in. Let's go and find somewhere."

"I will stay here," said Dregar, "and see that Framin is safe, and think about what we must do with him."

***

Since they had trapped him, Framin had tried to break through the energy around him, but every time he reached out and touched it he became weaker. It was as if the lattice itself was sucking the essence from him if he touched it. He had stopped and sat down, and started to think and examine his predicament.

They had taken him by surprise, and he was unprepared for their understanding of everything. No problem though, he would find a way. As he sat and looked at the problem, he realized that there may be a way to follow one of his lines to his Gouarong. If he established that link, then he would start to transfer his essence along the line and take up residence in that body. The fact that he would have to clear the essence of the host and therefore kill him didn't bother Framin at all. If he could manage to find the connection, that would be of no consequence.

He studied the lattice again, and this time instead of trying to push something through he went down to the lowest level of essence he knew. Once there he could see that what surrounded him did not behave like anything he had ever seen before—it seemed to be the exact opposite of how he expected everything to work. As he looked at the construction in detail, he began to realize that Elji had constructed it using what was present in the quantanium that Lhapso had found. This was antiessence, and

212

that was the flaw. Because they had sealed off the other plain, this construction had nothing to tether itself to or to sustain it. In other words, in this reality it was not real, or at least could not sustain itself for long—it had no connection. Very clever, he thought. He looked again at the construction, and could see that in certain tiny places it was beginning to break down.

He thought about it again, and realized that if he were to imagine his essence was made up of uncountable particles that were smaller than anything he knew and opposite to anything he could imagine, he might be able to push one through. If he could do that and connect with one of the lines to his Gouarong, he may be able to establish a connection and push himself along that line. It was certainly worth a try.

Wait, he thought. If I can get even one imaginable particle through, I can put everything I am in that one particle and then send it. Inside himself he dissolved everything that he was into one particle, leaving only enough to sustain his earthly form so that they would believe he was still there, and headed for the gap he imagined. He was through.

He cast about, looking for a connection to his Gouarong. The only thread left that he could discover was to Bethrod. All the others were gone. He rushed along his line. As he did he thought that this was not good news. The fact that his Gouarong were gone was something he would have to try and understand.

***

Bethrod recoiled—something assailed him at his very core. He recognized it straight away; it was Framin. He threw up a defense and the attack was recoiled.

***

Framin couldn't get in—Bethrod defended. It didn't

213

matter. Framin cast around and saw Bethrod's wife Kreanna; that would do. He pushed his essence into her and hid for now.

He had accomplished what he wanted—he was out. Now he would start; now he would revenge himself—but he would be patient…he had to be. He had lots of time now to plan and to think and to find out what had happened.

***

Bethrod looked round the room and searched back through his essence. Nothing. That was strange; he was certain he had felt Framin. But he could find no sign of him now. He stood, a little confused and worried, and then decided.

He needed to speak to Elji and the others, and needed to do it now. It was in any case time to plan how to move things along. First, though, he needed to see how Cloin and Naimer were getting on.

***

Framin was indeed content; he had evaded being discovered by Bethrod. He would watch from where he was. He had already cordoned off part of Kreanna's mind. She wouldn't know he was there until he needed her to know. His plan was simple. He would leak himself into her very slowly, bit by bit, and try and influence her without anyone noticing. He would make subtle changes, and by the time anyone noticed he would have some plans in place and it would be too late for anyone to do anything about it.

As he had listened and searched around in Kreanna's mind, he hatched a further plan that may well be his saving grace. They were losing a daughter. He had thought about shifting from Kreanna to Naimer or Cloin, but they were weak, and the possibility of them not surviving was high. While he could move from one to the next it took energy, and being

214

incarcerated in Elji's lattice had weakened him past the point he could do anything using force of will. He had used the last of his current strength on moving this way.

No, he would wait. He would influence Kreanna bit by bit and ensure that she nurtured a further child. Once that was done he would transfer his essence to the child. It would take years, but he had time. He had been patient for longer than most could remember, and a setback of a few tens of years was nothing to him. He would gather his power. He would move his essence into the unborn child and grow with it. Being of the bloodline of someone who had real power would offer him opportunities that he could exploit. He was more than happy to wait.

He started to plant the seed into Kreanna's mind—he was sure this would work.

**

Dregar was watching Framin from outside the lattice, and though he was unsure it was a good idea to keep him here, it was better than anything else he could think of. He had tried to penetrate the prison that bound Framin, but his abilities didn't seem up to the task. This gave him hope. He could see Framin inside the cage, but no matter how he tried he didn't seem able to reach him. Framin was just sitting, slouched inside, but he did seem to be alive. Dregar decided that considering the current circumstances, that was enough. He thought he might go and find the others and take some rest.

As he left the room he fashioned another layer of protective essence around the room, and hid it from sight by moving it just out of alignment in time and space. It was probably belt and braces, but he felt better having been able to do something.

Framin had been a blight on their plans for longer than he

cared to remember, and to have him where he was powerless was more than he could have hoped for when they started out on this plan.

It was time to relax a bit and take in some much needed food and rest. There was a lot to do and oversee, and a lot that he would like to hear from Elji. He was tired and pleased at the same time, and for now that would suffice.

He made his way up to the main palace area.

CHAPTER 27
THE KILDORAI

Bethrod and Kreanna made their way to the room where their son and daughter were being cared for. Standing over them was Tragarg and another of the Drendrak, one who had devoted himself to the healing of others.

"How are they both?" asked Bethrod.

"Cloin is slowly recovering," said Tragarg. "But we are worried about Naimer. There is little to no response from her. Being as she is part of the Drendrak, they have been collectively sending her healing, but she seems unable to receive any of it."

Zefari the Drendrak healer looked at them both. "I think that unless we can do something soon, we will be forced to take her graithe and ensure that she is preserved amongst the sect. It may well be the best that we can do. At least we will have her memories and her experience."

Kreanna sat beside her daughter and took her hand, and looked up at Bethrod. "We knew this may be a possibility, but I never thought it would actually come to pass. Is there nothing that can be done? She is so young, and has so much promise."

Tears were beginning to form in Kreanna eyes, and the raw pain could be felt in the room.

Zefari spoke. "There may be one chance," he said. "We could take her to one of the Kildorai. Their home is in the cold lands of the north, way beyond any place that is inhabited as we know it. They are a people who live as one with the essence of the planet and all its living things. They are healers by nature, and if they deem it fit that she should live, they may be able to return her to health. If they do she will have to denounce all family ties, and become a healer only to be found in times of great need. I have not had the grace to meet them or be trained by them, but I hear that their knowledge is unsurpassed in this."

"Do you know how to find them?" asked Kreanna.

"I know that there is believed to be one living at the foot of the hills to the east of the city," said Zefari. "No one has ever seen this, but it is legend that it is so. If it is told within the Drendrak, then it is more likely than not to be right. If you wish to do this, then we must take her and leave her in that place. If she is worthy she will be taken and healed. If not, she will either be eaten by whatever predator is around or she will die of starvation. It is said that none may stay with the offering, and the outcome will only be known after three days, if in the place of the one that is dying a tree of life has begun to grow. It is unmistakable—it is silver like the light of a full moon, and it bears golden tipped leaves that sing in the breeze. It will be a few feet tall, and will forever be a place of peace and tranquility."

"What have we to lose?" asked Bethrod. "We either sit and hope and perhaps lose what we have anyway, or we give this a chance. I cannot sit by and do nothing. What do you say, Tragarg?"

"I have heard this legend. It is part of our heritage of

knowledge, therefore in my mind it is real, though I have never seen it and there is risk. But as you say, what choice do we have?"

"We lose a daughter, but at least she will live. Our grief will be lessened knowing that," said Bethrod. "So, how do we accomplish this thing?"

"Tragarg and I will transport her to the place we believe she must be, and we will leave her there. Now is the time for you to say your goodbyes. Even if she is taken by the Kildorai, I doubt that you will see her again."

Tragarg and Zefari left them alone.

Bethrod and Kreanna were lost in their grief for Naimer. It was indeed not something any parent should feel, the loss of a child. Bethrod was saddened—even with all his knowledge, power, and planning he had not been able to stop this thing and protect those he cared for the most. She was, he knew, a force of good. Her brother would miss her, deeply. Their bond was strong, but Cloin was, if nothing else, a warrior, and he would bear his grief with pride as any warrior would. Bethrod's wife, though was, a different matter. She was strong, but was she strong enough to bear this loss?

He looked at her, and ached to be able to wind back the last few days and undo what had been done. He vowed there and then to do anything he could to make this right for Kreanna, and to make the world a better place for her and what was to come. He knew they would never forget Naimer, but over time the rawness of the loss might lessen.

"My love," he said. "Let's say goodbye—the longer we wait the harder for us and for her it will be."

He noticed that something had broken in Kreanna. He could feel a rift in her, as though some part of her was missing. She bowed her head, hugged her daughter, turned, and marched out.

Bethrod looked at Naimer. "I promise that with my last breath I will remember you, and I hope that one day you can return to us. You will always be in our hearts." He turned and left the room.

***

Tragarg and Zefari went back in, linked their hands, encircling Naimer, and Zefari let go a clear pure note. They faded.

The air was freezing cold, and they stood in at least three feet of snow. The trees all around them were bowing with the weight of the snow on the branches, and there was not another plant to be seen. They had come to the east of the city at the foot of the hills, where they thought one of the Kildorai lived.

Tragarg cleared an area for them and they laid Naimer on the ground. "Is there anything we should do?" he asked.

"No," said Zefari. "It is said that those of the Kildorai know when one is coming, and if they are needed they will come. Let's go—there is nothing more we can do."

They left her there.

***

From the trees came a tall figure. Her hair was as white as the snow that surrounded her. She walked across the snow, leaving almost no footprint, as if floating across the top. She stepped down and looked at Naimer, and smiled. Her face was long and elegant, regal looking, in perfect proportion to the rest of her. "Come, Naimer," she said. "It's time to go."

Naimer opened her eyes and stood. She took the woman's hand and they walked across the snow the same way the woman had come. As they walked, they faded from sight.

CHAPTER 28
SECRECY AND SALVATION

Bremen, Dregar, Elji, and Talisha were all sitting, each with their own thoughts, in the library room of Bremen's palace, waiting for Bethrod and Cloin. What had happened to Naimer had been relayed to them and they were saddened by the news, but hopeful that at least there was a possible path for her.

Bremen had told them of what had happened to Saloora, and each had voiced their sympathies and felt the loss on a personal level. What other losses had occurred so far was difficult to tell. Not all the information had come back to them, but they were sure that Bethrod would give them an update on the situation in each of the cities they had attacked.

Elji stood up and started to pace around. There was a great deal of planning to do, and he had yet to give each of them an overview on what he knew and what they must do going forward. Of all of the information, the fact that Elgred and Charina were now absent was going to come as the biggest shock to them all, though he suspected that Dregar knew more than he was letting on. Elji had weighed in his mind how much of what he knew he should divulge, and had decided that not everything need be told. Some things were best kept secret. He would not be telling them of the different futures he had seen for their world — he would just emphasis the importance of what they were about to embark upon.

When he stopped to think about the magnitude of what they were trying to do, it felt pretty hopeless. They had to set in motion things that would help to influence the world for thousands of years. They had to ensure somehow that the majority of the population heard the message of hope and love, and that the majority that took up that message of hope and love would influence others to join them. It was going to be a long, slow, laborious process. People were going to be very wary of trusting those that were seen as in charge of them. Most had been subjugated to vile acts and fed hopelessness for many years.

It wasn't just what happened now, though, that he was worried about. He would need to ensure that they had things and people in place that would be able to watch for any that tried to undo these plans, both now and for thousands of years. He really didn't have much of an idea right at this moment in time as to how they were going to accomplish such a task. He did know that he had good people with him, and that they would have to find many more good people to help them. They would have to recruit and swear to secrecy those that they recruited.

He had toyed with the idea of just showing as many people as possible the power he had. Show them how they could change things and have the things that they needed. Explain to them about the universal essence. But how to train them? And he was sure that if he just tried to tell everyone everything, many would brand him a lunatic, and yet others would turn such to their advantage and try to wrestle the strings of influence for their own advancement. No, that wasn't the way to go. They would have to make sure the message was subtle and real, and people could see real benefits from what they did and said.

He was feeling more than a little out of his depth in all of this, and felt used by Elgred and the others. He had little choice in his current situation, and they had definitely manipulated him into this position by not being as forthcoming as they could have been with information in the first place.

Gods! he thought, as that is what he had decided they were in the absence of any better term to describe them. Though they strove to do the best they could, it was very evident that they were not opposed to manipulating situations to try and bring about an end that they would like. Though they didn't see it, he was of the mind that each had an ego, and each wanted something to happen in the way they envisaged it. At least he thought they were concentrated on ensuring that his race survived and had the best possible opportunity of joining the universal all. So he had decided that it could be worse.

He wasn't sure that he understood their policy of no direct intervention despite the gravity of the situation that was occurring. It seemed to him that this would probably be the best method of ensuring things went how you wanted them to. Still, they had been around for all of time and had managed to bring millions of planets to fruition, and he was sure that even though they were in control there must be politics at play. He had seen some of it when he was on Talisha's home world and had had his vision, as he liked to call it.

He and the people here would have to be much more concerned with day to day activities, ensuring that things were in place to enable the best possible future for all of the race.

He and the people around him could not be distracted by the deeds of everything else in the universe. They must ensure the survival and evolution of this planet.

Now how to do that.

He was hungry, and he thought he could definitely do with a drink of some kind. The stronger the better, he thought.

"Bremen, while we wait is there any possibility of something to eat and drink? The stronger the better, I think."

"Of course, Elji." Bremen stood up to go and see about sorting it out just as Jawarat entered. "Ahhh, Jawarat," said Bremen. "Might there be some food and a good bottle or two of wine you could provide, please?"

"Of course, I shall see to it. I was just coming to tell you that Bethrod and Cloin have arrived and are on their way here."

"Thank you, Jawarat."

Bethrod and Cloin came into the library as Jawarat was leaving and came across to the others. They all embraced. It was clear that both were under pressure from what had happened to Naimer. There was a sadness in Cloin that could almost be felt.

"Thank you for coming," said Elji. "I know it's a difficult time, but we have a lot to do and a lot to speak about, so thank you."

"It's OK," said Bethrod. "To be honest with you, it will be good to understand what needs to be done and get busy doing it. I think it will help ease the sadness."

"It's good to see you are recovered, Cloin. Without your intervention I am almost certain none of us would be in the position we are now. Thank you."

"We are the lucky ones," said Cloin. "It's the likes of Saloora and Naimer who paid the ultimate price, and as in all battles I am sure there will be in the number of hundreds who gave up their life for a cause they know little about. People just doing what they see as their duty. I have been thinking about this a great deal, and I wonder if there might be a better way. A way where people know what it is they strive for."

"That," said Bremen, "is what we come to discuss."

Jawarat returned with others carrying food and wine. They placed it all on a table and left them to it.

Elji picked up the wine and poured everyone a glass. "To absent friends," he said, and took a good swallow of the wine.

"Absent friends," the others echoed.

Elji sat and leaned towards the table, and spooned himself some lamb and rice that was on a large platter in the middle. Taking up some flat bread, he began to eat. The others, seeing him, fell to the food, and soon they were all eating and drinking.

Dregar, who had been all but silent till this point, said "If you like, Talisha and I can give you the benefit of how our separate races have accomplished what we all are now about to try and achieve. While our circumstances will not be entirely relevant, they should at least give some food for thought." He looked around and everyone was nodding.

Talisha took that as agreement. "I will give you a brief history, as I don't think that our world parallels yours in many respects, if any, but it is still interesting. We, the Kuwali, started as a primitive desert race many hundreds of thousands of years ago. Our planet was unlike yours in that it could not sustain life in many places, and from what I can tell is about a quarter of the size. Most of the planet is a desert, and is uninhabitable by all but a few creatures that can live without water. Because of that we were never a race that is anywhere near as prolific in numbers as you are here. There were a few places round the edges of continents that sustained life. As we progressed each of these places found its own equilibrium in terms of numbers of people, and soon, being near the sea, they started to explore by building seafaring vessels. In each of the lands where the population grew we had a seam of the stone that was fed from the sea, and that is what we now make the galrass from. As this stone was discovered, we found we were able to converse with each of the other settlements with ease via the stone. Trade grew, and each shared in the bounty of the other. We fashioned rooms in the seams of stone, and began to learn from it. Once one of us had the knowledge it was passed from them to everyone else. That is how we gained knowledge about the universe and its workings. In sharing that knowledge, we each felt at peace, knowing that everyone was equal in the understanding of the all.

"Our history does not tell of wars or of greed, but of peace and love and sharing. As time passed and we learned more of the universe, we were contacted by others, and it was discovered that certain among us had the knack of putting all that was in the universe into a galrass. This took many, many thousands of years to accomplish, by which time our elders had been given all the knowledge they needed to understand the importance of what we did. As far as I know in the telling of the history we have never worshiped a god, but have cherished all living things, giving each equal weight and respect. I believe the difference to be that our people numbered in the tens of thousands, not the vast numbers you have here on this world."

"It's interesting," said Bremen. "You are right, it does not hold many parallels to what we have here. Nonetheless, it shows what can be achieved without greed and hate. It is the very core of what we have been trying to achieve here in Mehem. Slowly but surely we have been trying to ensure that the voice of love and good is the loudest heard, and that everyone understands the benefits of following that path. The problem we have is that we number a few amongst the multitude of people, and our message is just a small voice."

Dregar spoke up. "Our planet's history, though again, not entirely parallel to yours, does have some similarities. I am from a world called Quandium, and this world still exists, though there are less than a hundred of us left now. We have been a race for millennia in the universe, and have undergone many forms of evolution. Now we are not what you would consider to be corporeal beings, but we can manifest as such.

"My race, early on in its existence, became aware of the essence and how it could benefit them, and they rushed toward it. We made advances in what we knew very quickly, and soon became millions of people that possessed powers to construct and build devices that would be incomprehensible should I try to explain them to you. They were things that allowed us to travel to other worlds and create great healing. But all these things needed something to make them work—a source of great power. But that power also had the ability to cause massive destruction.

"My people became greedy in their growth, and some wanted to rule everything and conquer other worlds. Others wanted to tread more carefully and be at one with ourselves first. The differences in opinion caused wars, and in the end we all but destroyed ourselves with our creations. What was left of my world shunned all things, and went back to the basics of what the universal essence provided. From that we grew again as a people of compassion and understanding, and in the end we ascended to be what we are now.

227

"The biggest problem, as shown by our history, was making sure that the message we needed reached everyone to give them the opportunity to embrace all that is good. We failed, and that is why we nearly destroyed ourselves. If somehow we can achieve that here, then your race may reach its true potential and join in the universal family. How we do it I am not too sure."

It was an observation that each of them agreed with.

"There are some things I learned while all this was going on," said Elji. "There are those in the universe whose sole aim, like Framin, is to disrupt races from benefiting from the essence. Though I wasn't shown who they are, it seems that from the chaos they create they are able to fashion creations of their own, driven by greed and ego. We saw that with the black holes and the attempt to create a new concept of reality altogether. I hope that we have, for now, put a stop to that. Though with something that fundamental I am not sure we have seen the last of it.

"Here on this planet, because we seem to have potential, both the forces are strong, and as a race we have the ability to embrace either. We will not be seeing Elgred and Charina for a while, and with the sealing off of the black holes by Talisha using my galrass, there may well be a lessening of things we can access in the universe using the essence. Having two universes in existence at once, they told me, will cause some paradoxes. It is something we will have to deal with, and we don't know how it will affect us in the present. So we will have to think and watch. Though I haven't told you everything, one thing is for sure—we need to establish a society—a secret sect, if you like—that will watch the evolution of our kind and counteract anything that seems to be pushing the race toward hate and self-destruction.

"As well as that, I think we need to build a place that will bring people together to learn, and then send those people out to teach others. We have an opportunity now, with what Bethrod has accomplished in taking control of the cities that were overseen by the Gouarong.

"Framin could not have known, but in causing us to remove his hold on those cities, he has afforded us an opportunity to spread our teachings. We can use the Drendrak to be the cornerstone of the beginnings of something that preaches the path we must follow. Bremen, and his father before him, has already made great strides here in Mehem in showing how cooperation and kindness can bring benefits to people. This is the model we need to proliferate around the cities we now hold."

Bremen put down his wine. "We can use the palace here to create a place of learning. To teach those that want to learn to spread the word. I don't want the death of Saloora to be in vain. Her name, Ahhbreshemen, though I didn't understand it at first, makes sense now. Hers is the voice that will be heard, the voice of good, of love. She is the voice of me, of our teachings. She will be heard everywhere, and in every corner. Even though she is gone from here, I feel her. She will be the catalyst that enables us to spread the message."

They continued to talk and plan well into the night, Jawarat came and replenished the food and drinks.

"I think," said Cloin, "that I am for bed. It has been a very long and difficult few days. I need rest."

"Yes," said Elji. "That is by far the best suggestion we have had so far," he smiled. It was the first smile any of them had seen in a while. "In the morning you should return home and begin to help the Jalaria bring peace and prosperity to the cities."

Bethrod and Cloin stood up and made their way out of the room, Dregar followed. Talisha and Elji stood.

"You haven't told them everything, have you?" Talisha said.

"No," said Elji. "Some things are best kept for when they need to be told. We have all had enough pain and loss for now. Let's enjoy the possibilities of a future that we can believe in for now. Come on. Let's go and sleep."

"Sleep?" she said. "I am hoping that there may well be more than sleep involved."

Elji laughed at her and took her waist. "You may be the best thing that ever happened to me." As they walked he remembered the warnings that had come to him. *You will watch all those you love die.* He sighed. He just couldn't be concerned with that right now. Now was the time to grab whatever happiness was on offer.

CHAPTER 29
CONSOLIDATION

Harther was sitting in what he thought of as the crown room, because there was a huge throne in the shape of a crown at the head of a very large table. Vladoon and some of his men were sitting around him.

"What is the situation in the city now?" he asked.

"Since we wrested the portal away and the other portals dropped, the general populace is leaving us alone. Most of what is left of the defenders have fled the city — those that haven't we have rounded up in the barracks. We lost no more than a dozen men in the whole battle. The enemy didn't seem very ready to fight, and certainly was not aware that they were about to be attacked. It couldn't have gone much smoother than it did. In fact, many of the men feel a little cheated of a good fight."

"Well, get the men into the citadel and let's get some food and drink handed out. A good party after a conquest always cools hot heads. Make sure that we have room for people to stay, and make sure the men do not scour the city for any loot or women they might find. This is not our normal take over.

We need to be sure that after this is done we can control the city peacefully."

His men stood and went to do his bidding.

Vladoon looked at him. "I hear that there are men and women starting to gather outside the palace. Most of them are hungry and have been ill-treated. They are looking for whatever we can give them."

"Until we get Bethrod here and you can get clear instruction on what we are to do going forward, I think we might as well extend the celebration to the grounds of the palace.

Let's declare this day as a freedom day. Get plenty of food and drink sent out. Get a message to all in the city that they can come and feast at the hands of those that have freed them.

Make sure that we have men patrolling the streets in the capacity of peace keepers. If there are any inns around about, speak to them and see that they give free food and drink if they are able, and if they do that they can come and claim recompense for it."

Harther was having to think on his feet. He had never been in a position to rule somewhere without having to conquer the local people and instill fear into them so that they obeyed the new rule. He would wait for Bethrod and see what he had to say. Right now, though, he needed ale. He left the crown room and wandered into the palace to find some.

***

Jalad and Florin, along with some of their men, had liberated the City of Spires. The guard that had protected the palace and ruled the people with fear were driven off. There were cheers from the streets, and people were starting to spill out to speak and congratulate each other. There was a feeling here that he had not seen in a very long time.

As he walked the streets to the docks, Jalad could see that people were singing and drinking. News had spread fast; he hoped that the celebration didn't deteriorate into looting and general debauchery. When given freedom all of a sudden, people were apt to push that boundary too far.

He had left Florin in charge at the palace, and he was overseeing the policing of the city so they were sure it was in safe hands. He had other things on his mind. He wanted to be sure that he could return as many children as he could back to the city. It had lost its life since most of them had left, and he now wanted to get that back.

He was determined that his city, this city—the City of Spires—would return to its former glory and be known as a place of worship and beauty as it had been in times past. He had been told that friends of Bremen and Saloora would soon be here to help him look after the city, and positions and responsibility would be shared. He wasn't one for authority; he just needed to be sure that people were free. Still, he would do what he could, and if there was an opportunity for him and his family to prosper in this new venture he wouldn't pass that up.

First things first though. The children....

***

Bethrod and Cloin had returned to their city, and along with Tragarg had spoken to the Drendrak in each of the other cities, relaying the plans. They had also dispatched another of his trusted generals, along with his Drendrak, to the City of Spires, and they would be there soon.

Bethrod and Tragarg had started to visit the cities themselves to ensure that his men knew what was expected of them to reinforce the message. The plan was to be very simple. Free the people. Let them recommence commerce, and build up a city based on freedom and choice. Start to spread the teachings of Bremen, those of tolerance, kindness, sharing, and love.

They would need to understand what each city was capable of in terms of what they could produce from the land, or make and set up chains of commerce between the cities. To do this each of the men that Bethrod had put in charge was to make connections with traders and merchants in the cities. To understand who owned and controlled what and ensure that each was willing to help build what would be profitable trade.

In each city there was to be built a temple to the goddess Ahhbreshemen. They were to start to recruit acolytes. Bremen had sent one of his most trusted students to each city, and they would begin the sharing of knowledge and truth.

Cloin had not joined his father on the journeys. He was recovering—he was not as strong as he'd thought. And in any case, he needed to create a bond with a new Drendrak, his sister now having left them.

Finding a new Drendrak would not be easy. That bond was made very early on in childhood. It was rare, but not unknown, that such bonds were created later in life. He had need to go to the lodge of the Drendrak and start the ritual to see who he could bond with.

***

Kreanna was sitting in her and Bethrod's room. Since his leaving she had become more and more reclusive, and though it had only been a very short time, she missed him. The loss of Naimer had struck her very hard, and as she sat with only her thoughts an idea had gathered in her mind. She knew he would be home at any moment, and she was going to discuss it with him.

She heard talking outside the door, then it opened and in

234

walked her husband. She marveled at the sight of him as she did every time she saw him. When he was near she always felt safe.

She crossed the room to him and kissed him. "What news of the cities?" she asked.

"All is going according to plan up to now," said Bethrod. "It is still the very early days, but we are making progress. I am sure that there will certainly be many challenges to face, but we have made a start." He smiled at her. "You look tired, Kreanna."

"I am tired. While you were away there was a lot for me to take care of here. Since we started all this we do not seem to have much time. I have been thinking. In all of this loss, I think we need something to celebrate. We have discussed this before, and now seems as good a time as any. Much of the pain and evil is gone, and before we get too much older." She looked up at him, and he looked at her with a quizzical look on his face.

"What are you asking, Kreanna?"

"Bethrod, I want another child. I want a child that will grow up in a more peaceful world, not one that knows war and pain and death."

***

"A child," he said, startled, and then he smiled at her. "I thought our parenting days were over. But you know, you may be right—we deserve some happiness and chaos," he laughed. He picked her up. She was as lithe as the first day he had met her despite her being somewhat older. He had never strayed from her. She had been his rock and his foundation for years. He loved her now as he had the first time he had seen her, and his need for her had never diminished.

He carried her to the bed, and was about to lay her gently

down when he changed his mind. He twirled around with her, threw her on the bed, and leapt on top. They both burst out laughing.

"It's been a long time," she said.

"Yes, it has," he replied, and kissed her.

***

Bremen was busy overseeing the building of the place of learning. They had chosen to extend the back of the palace so that any who joined could make full use of his library and all the facilities that were already in place. He had been excited to start this journey, and even more pleased that they had all decided to dedicate this building and all the new temples in the other cities to Ahhbreshemen. He could hear her in his mind saying that such a thing was nonsense — she was not worthy. He laughed out loud, and some of the workers turned to see what the noise was. He held up his hand in apology and walked back to the palace.

There was so much to do. He had started to send his students out into the lands to search for new and eager converts. Those that he could teach the ways and tell the stories to so that they could go out and spread the word. His fervent hope was that he would find some that he could share his entire knowledge of the essence with. From those he might find one or two that he, Elji, and Talisha could trust to become one of the few that knew everything. One they could entrust the future of the race to.

It was a bold undertaking, but at present, following everything that had happened, it was all going as well as could be expected.

He saw Dregar in the library, and entered to have a word with his friend. Dregar had undertaken the task of trying to coordinate the many lines of communication that were needed to coordinate an effort that spanned the majority of the globe. Since the release of the galrass into the black hole, many were finding it difficult to manipulate the essence in quite the same way as they used to. Bremen had found that he was unable to transport himself for great distances. Dregar seemed to have no such trouble. He still just twirled his stick and he was gone.

"How is it going, my friend?" he asked Dregar.

"It is going," said Dregar. "If I had known how difficult a task this was going to be, I don't think I would have volunteered quite so quickly." He laughed. "I am not sure I have the knack for keeping everything in order. I am fine with relaying messages, but I am not sure I have the ability to order all the information properly to make sure that nothing is missed. Do you perhaps have someone that I can entrust some of the more mundane sorting of information to? Someone like a clerk?"

"I do indeed," said Bremen. "I will speak to Jawarat, and he will send someone to you." Bremen smiled at him. "I suspect you are getting itchy feet? I don't think I have ever known you stay in one place for such a long time. Once we have someone to help, why don't you go and see Elji and Talisha and see how they are getting on?"

"Good idea," said Dregar. "Now, where is this person?"

Bremen laughed again. "I will get on it straight away."

CHAPTER 30
A SECRET BEST KEPT.

Elji and Talisha were sitting in the room they used the most. It was large, and at one end was a fireplace that took up most of the wall. It had an array of pots and utensils that hung from various hooks or stood on shelves. The room itself was constructed from wood and stone from the quarry outside the village where Elji's mother and brothers lived. As such it had a quality that in certain light it gave different hues and aspects. The rest of the building had an open plan, and was based around the beits that were used on Talisha's home world. The only difference was that certain facets were closed in with the stone. The climate on the inlet was warm, and the arrangement gave a cool and pleasant place to live.

They had chosen a cove on the shoreline of a great sea, to the east of the city of Mehem, which reminded them both of the home of the Kuwali. It was uninhabited for many miles surrounding it, and seeing as there was no one to dispute their claim, they had arranged that some form of deeds be drawn up by Jawarat that stated they were the owners.

They had stayed long enough at Mehem to ensure that things were starting to progress in the way they had all agreed. It had taken them days and days to discuss how best to go about creating a lasting legacy for the future of their race, but in the end everything had been decided and the plans were put into motion.

Bremen was to be the utmost authority on all things to do with the spiritual wellbeing of the people, and seeing as the city of Mehem had a structure that seemed to work, this model was to be used for all the other cities. The Drendrak and their lords were to rule in each city, with Bethrod as the overarching ruler. He, in turn, would consult with Bremen. The Drendrak and the temples that were being created would hold a kind of senate, and report back to the central temple in Mehem on how things were going. They had tried to keep things as simple as possible.

It had become apparent very quickly that while as a group they knew about ruling and the wellbeing of the people, the commerce and coordination of goods, materials, building, and general coordination of building an empire was beyond them all. Jawarat and Tragarg had come into their own in this aspect, as each of them had managed the building and coordination of their own cities for decades.

Jawarat was given the responsibility of recruiting and setting up structures that enabled commerce and trade, and a body of people who understood and managed this. Tragarg was tasked with ensuring that building and transport was robust. Each of them had grumbled as much as they felt they could get away with at the tasks they were given, but it was apparent very quickly that they were adept at such things.

That had left Elji and Talisha, and in some respect Dregar, to think about and plan for the future. Those three were just the beginning of the group, but Elji had full intention of bringing Cloin and his Drendrak, once he was chosen, into their group.

He and Dregar had discussed the visions that Elji had seen in the temple of the four at great length. Dregar had tried to clarify for him some of what he had seen and describe the possible structures and growth of the race as he saw it over time, based on what Elji had told him.

Elji was certain that they needed a secret society that had influence on all the bodies of people that controlled things. He needed to ensure that if there was any circumstance where the populace was being influenced again by dark forces, he could counteract it. On listening to the stories of Dregar, he became more and more worried that over time the greed of people would outweigh their want to be part of something that was good. His only chance to influence that was to make sure that he could get information on how progress was being made, and in which direction it was going.

He also knew that even though for now they had thwarted Framin's plans, there were others in the universe whose sole aim was to try and turn all races to the path of darkness. As the four had said to him, "There can be no light without darkness, and no love without hate." It was something he feared more than anything.

The other things that occupied much of his thoughts were how the unleashing of a second universe within a universe was going to affect everything; and what of the quantanium and the black holes?

Elji sat back and let out a sigh.

"You're thinking too much again," said Talisha.

"I am," he said. "There is so much to think about, so much I don't know, so many things that are unpredictable."

"You can't plan for everything," said Talisha. "Some things you are not meant to know until they happen. We have a saying—it is 'Inshuniv.' It means 'in the hands of the universe.' Things will be what they will be. It is a good saying, and it is worth listening to. It will lighten your load till the time you need to worry about it. In your talks with Elgred and the others, it must have been obvious that nothing can control everything. We can only make the best of what we have and what we want. There will always be those that oppose that, and we will deal with that when the time is right."

"You are a very wise woman," said Elji. "It is no wonder your people live in such peace." He smiled at her. "Even so, we deal with something different here than your world does, and we must do everything we can to ensure we follow the right path. Even if we can't control everything we, must influence what we can. Sometimes I think life would have been much more simple as a boy in a village, with no knowledge and just living my life as it would be."

"If that had happened," said Talisha, "you would never have met me, and we would not be about to become parents."

Elji had returned to his thoughts again, but his head snapped up when he heard her words. "Parents?" he said. "What do you mean, parents? How is that possible?"

"If you don't know how it's possible," she said, "I worry about your understanding and shepherding of the universe." She laughed at him.

"I didn't mean it like that," he said, laughing with her. "Parents?" he asked again.

"Yes, parents."

He came to her and knelt down, taking her face in his hands. "So much has happened, so much to do, and now so much joy

241

to look forward to." He smiled the biggest smile she had seen yet. He lowered his head onto her lap and she stroked his hair.

"You will be a good father," she told him.

He lifted his head and looked at her. "I hope so."

At that he pulled her up from the chair and started to dance around with her. They were laughing and crying all at once.

Dregar entered the room. "Am I disturbing something?"

"Dregar," said Elji. "I am to be a father!"

Dregar smiled at them both. "It is always surprising to me, and sobering, that even in the midst of such turmoil the universe sends us signals of hope. And what could be more hopeful than new life. Let's drink," he said. "Let's celebrate."

"Now that is a good idea," said Talisha, and she left to bring some wine.

"To what do we owe the pleasure of this visit?" asked Elji.

"It was Bremen's idea. He could see that I was sinking under a mountain of organizing, so he suggested I come and find you and have a rest. I thought it was a good idea. There are still things that I need to understand, and I am itchy to get travelling again and need to know what I can do for you."

"We need to create a secret society here that watches all things. We need people we can trust, people who have skills. We can teach them everything we know of the essence — how to manipulate it, and how to use it to great advantage. I want this to be separate from what Bremen and the others do. Knowing what we know about the possible futures, I think it's important we have someone outside, watching and helping. If you need to travel I think that you should. Find and recruit people that you think might be what we are looking for. You can send them here and we will teach them. When Cloin is ready I am going to invite him here. He will be an asset to us."

"Well," said Dregar. "I found you, didn't I? I nurtured Saloora. I don't see why I can't find others. It is exactly what I like to do. I am a wanderer—I don't like being stuck to one place. I will gladly help. That news has cheered me up. I was beginning to feel I might begin to get old," he laughed, and Elji laughed with him. They both knew that Dregar was thousands of years old. "What should we call this secret society of yours?" asked Dregar. "And how are you going to fund such an enterprise?"

"A name," said Elji. "I hadn't thought we might need a name. We should call ourselves the Essaria—yes, I think that will do. As far as funding goes, Bethrod has said that he can manage to give us what we need to begin. I did take the opportunity to visit a couple of worlds that were early in their formation, and I brought back some precious stones—diamonds, sapphires, that sort of thing. I think we have enough to be considered very wealthy indeed. And if I need more…well, I will just make another visit. There has to be some advantages to understanding how things are created. We will need vast resources to continue this society for thousands of years, so I thought it best we be as independent as possible."

Talisha returned with wine, and they all settled down around the fireplace.

"How fares Framin?" asked Elji.

"As far as I can tell he is OK," said Dregar. "He still refuses to engage with anyone. He does nod and grunt every now and then, but mainly he does not interact with anyone. There are logistical problems. We have not been able to feed him as yet, as no one can get through the lattice you set up. I am not too worried about that—I know he can sustain himself for decades without food. He is an elemental being, and eating is only something he needs do to keep his earthly form alive. Still, it

243

would be good if you could think of a way we can offer him sustenance. It may be a way we can interact with him more and try and change his thinking."

"I will think on that," said Elji. "Though I don't trust him at all. He is very dangerous, and we shouldn't underestimate him. I still worry about the depth of involvement he had with the essence from the black holes, and though Elgred and the others told me that the line of reality we were on was the reason that Lhapso was involved, I get the feeling they were leaving out some vital information. I understand the concept of fixing the timeline by removing something and thereby setting something on a different path, but I know that the four are not subject to such things. So my question is, why did they think the subterfuge around Lhapso and Ichancha was necessary? Was it really to draw people into the situation that may not have been? Or was there something deeper than that involved? They are, as far as we know, the most powerful entities in the universe, or in any reality we can imagine. So why would they want to involve us in something they could have resolved themselves?"

"If you ask me, they are primarily concerned with ensuring that planets and races become self-managed," said Dregar. "They have far too many things going on. They have created more than they can manage. It is why they enlist the help of others. It is why there is a council to help the evolution of planets and people. I think they deliberately engineered a situation that would have the most beneficial outcome for them, and would allow them to have as little long term involvement as possible. I have known them for a long time, and I know that they don't do things just for the need to do them. There is always a reason and a plan."

"That is what worries me," said Elji. "The fact that they play

244

with lives and planets as if they were toys. It's worrying. In any case, let's talk of more pleasant things for now. Of late our conversations have been very deep, and there has to be time for some good news and some less in-depth discussions."

Talisha filled their glasses again. "Let's just enjoy the peace we have right now before we embark again on something that will need all of our attention."

They looked out from the room and watched the sun going down across the lake. It was casting a red glow that filled them with warmth and comradery.

"How I wish the alhitan were here," said Talisha, "How I wish we could hear them singing."

"There will be a time for us to return and hear them again," said Elji.

"If you like," said Dregar, "I can take you to a world where the notes of the universe are the language that is used for everything. They compose their songs to create such beauty it's almost unimaginable. I have been there no more than twice. It is a very difficult place to leave, and if you are not careful you can get lost in their songs forever. There are many places in the universe that would amaze you. Though I have to admit, the songs of the Kuwali and the alhitan come close to being one of the best experiences. You should go and visit before everything starts to become too complicated again."

"First let's get everything in motion, and then we will go." Elji looked at Talisha, and her face was alight with joy.

They sat and talked long into the night, and were still sitting when the sun rose. It was the dawning of a new age. The beginning of something that could be the future of everything, and they were firmly at the center of it all.

CHAPTER 31
SHADES OF DARKNESS.

Kreanna was walking through the palace towards the main hall. She felt wonderful. Her husband had been attentive, and they had spent some time just enjoying each other's company. It was a much-needed respite amongst the sadness and chaos of organizing everything. She stopped and put her hand on her stomach. Strange, she thought. I know that feeling, I remember it, but it can't be—it's been less than a week. She shrugged off the feeling and continued on her way. Impossible, she thought. Not yet—I wouldn't know yet. But deep in her mind she knew.

***

Framin was slowly transferring his essence into the growing embryo inside Kreanna. He was accelerating the rate at which the brain was being developed; he wanted to transfer all of himself as soon as possible. The rate of growth of this child would not be altered in any way. He couldn't afford to arouse any suspicion. When it was time and this child was born, he would be in full control of it, and though it might take years and years to be able to utilize the child, he would ensure that he

246

used every advantage he could gain.

He was content—well, as content as he could be under current circumstances. He still raged at the thought that Elji had managed to nullify him with such ease—he was going to be someone to watch. Still, he didn't need to think about that now; it was time to grow.

***

Kreanna stopped again. This time she had definitely felt a cramp, but it had passed as quickly as it had come. She sighed. Wishful thinking, that's what it was. But there was nothing wrong with that.

As she walked she started to think about Naimer. She hoped that she was safe and well. A new baby would never replace what she had lost, but it would make the pain more bearable.

Stop it, she thought. There you go again, believing something before it has even happened.

She entered the main hall and could see Bethrod and Cloin deep in conversation, looking over some charts. She went across, kissed her husband, and stood by her son. He had been away for a while at the lodge of the Drendrak, finding someone he could bond with.

"Did you manage to find your Drendrak?" she asked.

"Yes, Mother," he said. "We have held the ceremony, and now we are bonded. His name is Dravood. It was an easy choice—we were drawn to each other immediately. It was as if there were some of Naimer's essence in him. Though I know that can't be, it is nice to think it possible."

"If you had not been a warrior you could have been of the Drendrak," Karenna said. "You have a knowing of people's feelings and thoughts. It is a gift—you should trust it more."

"I'm pleased you are here," he said. "I was going to come

247

and find you. I am going to go and join Elji and Talisha. They have need of me, and I have a need to be busy."

"Oh! When do you leave?"

"I was just going to finish my conversation here and then be on my way." He smiled down at her. "Don't be so sad, Mother. You are used to us coming and going, and there is much to do."

She looked back at him, smiled, and said, "Yes, yes. It's just…." She let the sentence fall. I think I will mention something to Bethrod tonight, she thought. We need some good news.

Chapter 32
One last time

As it had done every morning, the sun rose, bright and hot, and the slight breeze ruffled the hangings at the window. He looked back at the bed and Charina was still lying there. Elgred turned back to the window.

How he would miss this. In all his realities he loved this one the best, and he enjoyed being one of them more than any other he had known.

He felt Charina's arm slide round his chest and he turned and smiled.

"Are you sure I can't persuade you to just give up everything and live like this forever" she asked him.

He laughed. "Nothing would give me greater pleasure. There is something about being human that is just so connected to everything that it makes your soul sing. That this race forgets and overlooks this is still astonishing to me. Why they can't feel the deep connection makes it seem like something we did wrong when we first created them. I hope that our interference so far has not hurt too many, and it will set them on the right

249

path. I have never liked manipulating the life forms we create; it just feels so wrong."

"We do what we must," said Charina. "And that is all we will ever do. Now, if I can just persuade you to come back to that bed?" She raised an eyebrow at him. He looked at her again and she was indeed beautiful, alluring in every way.

"Coffee and breakfast, though," he said. "I can't leave without one more coffee and one more breakfast."

"Bed first. Then coffee and breakfast, and then we will leave."

He gave in.

Colin Lives just outside the city of York in the beautiful Yorkshire country side. He has been married for 32 years and has two children and grandchildren. He has been acting and singing on stage since he was a teenager and still today performs at the large theatres in the region both acting and singing in lead roles.

He is a gym enthusiast and has competed in natural bodybuilding competitions and also engages in many sports such as Badminton, Squash and Bouldering. He has two dogs which keep him busy walking through the countryside.

Before settling in Yorkshire, he was brought up between the Middle East, where his parents worked in the Oil Industry and spending the rest of the time in the UK at boarding school. This is where his love for words came from and he has written poetry for many years.

He now has the time to pursue his passion of writing and has written his first book in a fantasy series that he says has been in his head for longer than he cares to remember.

www.colsinclair.com
https://www.facebook.com/authorcol/

Lightning Source UK Ltd.
Milton Keynes UK
UKHW011813090619

344072UK00001B/387/P

9 781629 899398